Also From Second Wind Publishing
by George Wright

Yaweta

Redstone

America Reborn

The Runaway

By

George Wright

Cut Above Books
Published by Second Wind Publishing
Kernersville

Cut Above Books
Second Wind Publishing, LLC
931-B South Main Street, Box 145
Kernersville, NC 27284

For information regarding bulk
purchases of this book, digital purchase
and special discounts, please contact the
publisher at
www.secondwindpublishing.com
Cover design by LeJoy Rothe
Manufactured in the United States of
America
ISBN 978-1-935171-04-1

This book is dedicated to my good friend Terry Bender who not only encouraged me to write, she proofread it and helped me in many ways in the production of this account of my life as a child.

These things could not be done in this day and age but what you are about to read happened.

Let me begin this story with a piece written by my good friend and mentor on the occasion of my birthday.

APRIL FOOL by TERRY BENDER

I know a man who was born on this day
At least this is the day he has chosen.
He took the name of the people
Who took him in and
Shaded to blend.
He just kept on
Moving
Forward,
Then step by step
Broke into a run,
Moving from train
To town
To farm.
He fed himself
And others too
And didn't let life
Slow him down.
I came upon him
Late in his life and
He's thrilled me with his tales.
For a boy who came with nothing,
Not a name, nor a birthday, not even
A clue, he has grown into one marvelous Man

1.

Have you ever heard the one about the traveling salesman and the farmer's daughter?

"It seems this traveling salesman's car broke down and he went to this farm house. Well, the farmer had this daughter, etc. etc." There are more farmers' daughter jokes than there are farmer's daughters. I think I have heard every one of them. When I was a kid, I never thought any of them were funny. Once you have been told a few thousand times, that you are the result of one of those jokes; you have an inclination not to find humor in them.

Then there are April Fools jokes. When the day you celebrate your birthday happens to be on April first, April Fools jokes, and tricks, are not particularly funny. After you have been told that you are an April Fools joke that was played on your parents a few hundred times, you tend to loose your sense of humor.

Have you ever heard of a "doorstep baby"? Well, I'm one of them. It doesn't happen often in this day, and age, but back during the Great Depression, before the Second World War, it was a lot more common than most people realize. Desperate people do desperate things. It was not that uncommon for a family that could not provide for their children to leave one, or more, of them with another person. Sometimes the other person did not know they had been "selected". A prosperous looking farm, darkness and a doorstep was all it took.

I don't know if that is what happened to me, or not. All I know is what the Wrights told me. George and Mary Wright, of Farmers Branch, Texas, told me that they got out of bed on April first 1938 and found me sitting on their front porch.

I have a memory, or a vivid dream, that haunted me... I am riding in a car. There are three other kids in the back, with me. A man and a woman are in the front. All of the participants are of the Caucasian race. They park the car beside a road. In a field, just off the road, is a single tree with a circular fence around it. Inside the fence are two bears. One bear is climbing the tree. I am crying as though I am frightened.

The only other piece of evidence is that whenever I asked, "Where am I from?" My English was corrected and I was told, "You're from Venus". This was never explained. I grew up thinking it was a joke of some kind. Many years passed before I learned that Venus is a town in Texas. It is just possible that they were referring to the town, rather than the planet. It may have been the truth.

At the time (1938) Venus, Texas, was on the decline. The depression had hit the community hard, and many permanent residents were leaving. In addition, there used to be a "shanty" town beside the railroad tracks as well. That is where itinerant farm workers came to live during the harvest season. Cotton was the main crop in the area.

When I was approximately fifty-four years of age I visited that town with my wife. Immediately upon arrival, I began describing what the town looked like many years earlier. I told her how the old board sidewalk in front of the grocery store would make noise when you ran down it. I came back another time and found some old books in the Senior Center. There were many pictures of the town, taken during the late "thirties". I had described the town perfectly. It does make me wonder...With the one possible exception, my earliest memories are of my home in Farmer's Branch. Farmer's Branch is now a part of the Dallas Metroplex, but when I was young there were farmers in the area.

The Wrights were good to me, but it was obvious that they were not my real parents. The Wrights, I believe, were from Ethiopia, or that region. Their skin was very dark. I hesitate to say "black". Mother Wright taught me that there are no "black" people, only brown people of various shades. When you think about it, she was entirely right. I was very conscious of my light skin coloring. Every summer I would try my best to become dark, "like my parents". It took a lot of patience, on Mother Wright's part to deal with my skin coloring problem.

I remember walking across a plowed field behind "Big George". He strode across the field with ease, but my little legs were not long enough. I had to work hard to keep up. It is one of my fondest memories. We were "buddies". Wherever he went, I wanted to go too. I admired that man, as only a son can admire his father.

Big George was what everyone called George Wright, and with good reason. He must have been six feet, six inches tall and built like a bulldozer. I once saw him in a fight, if you could call it that. It was then that I knew why very few people messed with that gentile man.

I was in the downtown area, near a bar, when three drunken men began go pick on me and call me names. They told me to get out of their neighborhood. One of them "cuffed" me and said "get out of here, white boy." That was a bad mistake. Evidently they didn't know that I was Big George's boy. He happened to walk up at that very moment. I started crying, as five-year-olds will do. I saw Big George pick that man off the ground and throw him against a building. The other two attacked, but one blow to each of them put them to sleep for a while. The whole incident happened in less than one minute, but it seemed like a lot longer. Big George just took care of the situation, took me by the hand, and said "let's go home son". He usually called me "boy". It was one of the few times I remember him calling me "son".

I got my name because of "Mother Wright". She always called her husband "Big George", and I was, "Little George". She used to watch us as we worked around the farm. Big George worked, and I got in the way. She seemed to get a big "kick" out of seeing us together. She was only about five feet tall, and well rounded. She was the best cook I have ever had the pleasure to meet. It has been over sixty years, and I can still smell the fresh bread, the apple pies, and the cinnamon rolls. If my real parents had wanted me to be well treated, and fed, they could not have picked a better family.

When V.E. day came it was the year I first heard a firecracker. One of the local farm boys came out to the farm throwing them out of the window of his car. He was as drunk as I have ever seen a man, and ecstatically happy. At first, I thought he was shooting, until I saw what he was doing. He kept yelling about the Germans surrendering. As I look back, I realize why he was so happy, he was "draft age". That day was know as "V.E." day for many years, but now few people know when it happened. I was hardly aware of the war. I knew about it, naturally, but it never affected me much.

We seldom left the farm during the first five years, or so. Consequently, I grew up alone. I helped around the farm, as much as a little kid can help. I fed the chickens, hoed the garden, gathered eggs, helped in the kitchen, among other things. It was when the Wrights thought I was old enough to go to school that the trouble started. I was not with them when they registered me with the local school as a six-year-old (their guess). Therefore it was assumed that I was of the same race. It was quite a surprise, when a "white" boy showed up in an all "black" school. Only the teachers were "white". Until then, I had never met another person of my own race. I had seen one, occasionally, but not up close.

The first day of school was interesting. If the Wrights had not interfered, they would have sent me to another school, clear across town. It would have been too far to walk.

After school was out for the day, a group of six boys persuaded me to accompany them to pick up a bunch of beer bottles so we could trade them in for money. We were under a railroad trestle when they "beat up on me". That was my introduction to school. I had at least one fight a day, and sometimes more, for a few weeks. Eventually, I learned how to dodge those boys. Those six were the only ones who really resented me. Not many people became friendly. Most of them just ignored the little "white" boy.

As I look back, I realize that those boys were really not very bright. After the first couple of days they always waited in the same spot next to an alley, for me to pass. There was a small building behind the bigger buildings along the main street. This building had a narrow passage all around it, about four feet wide. They waited there. I would walk up to the building, as though I was going to walk right into their "trap", then I would dash down the alley. I had made friends with the man at the Safeway store. He would let me go in his back door and out the front. He stopped the other boys from entering. The ruse never failed to work. All those boys needed to do, was to wait at the other end of that narrow passage.

I did very well in school. Mother Wright had been teaching me at home. I think she must have been a teacher at one time. Both of the Wrights spoke perfect English, as only people from Africa who have studied English speak it. She taught me subjects that I never got in school until much later, like history, geography, and the more advanced mathematics, such as multiplication and division.

It was after I started school that things changed. Times were good, and the farm was making money. With more money to spend, the Wrights began to "celebrate" quite frequently. It was then that I learned to cook for myself, or not eat at times. I learned how to do housework and a lot more of the farm work. I took care of things when the Wrights were not there to do it. By the time I finished the third grade they were either alcoholics, or nearly so. I became a caretaker when they were "feeling bad". I never minded. My life changed forever the summer I turned nine by their count.

2.

It was June. School had been out for a while and summer was just getting started. One evening we had visitors. It was strange because it was the first time I had ever seen "white" people in the house, other than an occasional worker. These people drove a fancy car, wore suits, and looked important. I heard the argument from my room.

They were going to take me away and put me in an orphans' home. To me, that was just like saying they were going to put me in jail.

There was a "white" man staying in the barn. He had come around a couple days earlier and asked to work for some food. Big George asked him to stay a few days and help with some fences, and barn repairs. The man was a Hobo, named Al Corn. We had done a lot of work together and had become friendly. I call him a man, but he must have been all of eighteen at the time. As far as I was concerned, he was an adult.

I sneaked out of my bedroom window and went to the barn. When I told Al what was going on, he said, "Go get your things, but not much, and let's get out of here. I was in one of those places once."

Five minutes later I had climbed back into the house, gotten some clothes, my twenty-two rifle, and about two dollars I had saved, and left. I was too frightened to cry, but I wanted to burst out in tears and beg those people to let me stay. I was so emotionally upset that my stomach hurt.

We went directly to the railroad tracks and caught the first train.

The very first night on the road, we slept in a boxcar, with three rough looking men. The train was moving north, away from Farmers Branch. Everyone was making themselves as comfortable as possible. I, for one, could not find comfort. I sat in a corner, as far away from the others as I could get. Al sat with me for a little while, with one arm across my shoulders. After a few minutes he asked if I was alright, so I told him everything was fine. I lied. I was scared to death. The orphan's home those people were talking about sounded pretty good right then.

Al went over to talk to the three men, while I sat there with my knees pulled up under my chin, and watched. Tears began to run down my cheeks as I quietly cried. My whole world had gone to pieces. It would not be the last time.

The men were as dirty as any I had ever seen. Big George got dirty in the field, but it was different. These men were grubby. Their hair was long and tangled like they hadn't seen a barber in a year, and didn't know a comb from a pitchfork. They had not shaved in a long time, but they didn't really have beards. They were just unshaven. All of them wore jeans and work shirts that had not seen a washing in months. Their shoes were worn, scuffed, and dirty. I could see holes in the soles of most of them. The men looked mean, to me, and that made my imagination run wild.

After what seemed like hours, but was only a few minutes, Al came back to where I was sitting. He said that I had better get some sleep. He made a pillow out of my coat and had me lay down about three feet from him. Before long Al and all three men were snoring. I could not sleep. Fear, emotion, and imagination kept me awake. The boxcar door was open and the moonlight caused the shadows to dance. My mind told me they hid all kinds of things. I lay there listening to the clatter of the wheels as they hit each joint in the rails. I felt every movement as the boxcar swayed back and forth.

About an hour had passed when I saw one of those fearsome men looking at me. He got up and started toward me. I just knew that man was going to do something terrible. I thought he might beat me and throw me out the door of the moving train. My imagination was running wild. I even thought he might eat me. I did not dare move. My eyes must have been as big as saucers as I stared back at him, not even blinking. He knelt down and placed his own blanket over my trembling body, then his hand ruffled my hair and a gentle voice said, "Sleep good, boy". I knew I was with friends because of that.

I slept like a baby.

When Al shook me awake, the sun was shining. He asked how I had slept. I said fine and then carried the blanket over to the open door and shook it out. I folded it neatly and took it over to the man. I said "thank you sir".

He looked down at me and grinned. "My name is `Rails', because I have been on them so long". He pointed to one of the others, "He's `Boxcar', and this other man is `Gondola'. None of us has a real name. Most Hobos don't. I think we'll call you `Caboose' cause that's the smallest car on the train"

I learned a lesson that I have never forgotten. Dirt doesn't make a man bad! I guess one might say that this was the beginning of an education in living. We lived together in that boxcar for two days. We shared what food we had. Most of it was dry bread and one man had a big hunk of cheese. My fear of the unknown became a sense of great adventure. My only remaining fear after that was that I would be caught and put in a "jail" called an orphanage. I missed my foster parents, but the resilience of youth helped me adjust. I knew that, if I went back to the farm, I could not stay. I would be in the Orphan's home.

Rails and his two friends left us. They headed to Chicago, but we were interested in going to a job Al said he knew about in Montana. Rails gave me the army blanket he had used to cover me with that first night, as a parting gift. I still had it, nearly ten years later, when I went back to visit the folks. I found a marker once and wrote on the corner, "To Caboose from Rails". That battered old army blanket, and my old twenty- two rifle, were part of what I lost when I was forced to leave everything after the "folks" died.

When Al and I got to Montana that first summer we didn't get to work at the ranch Al had in mind, but we did get work at a neighboring one. The first rancher had just hired a man. He said his neighbor needed a man, but he doubted he would hire one with a kid. We tried anyway. It was haying time. They put me to work cleaning up under the stacker and running the stacker team.

The stacker was an "overthrow" type. They used a "buck rake" to bring in a pile of hay. A buck rake is an old car, or jitney, with tines fastened on the front of it. The buck rake would deposit its load on the tines of the stacker. Then the stacker team raised, by the use of pulleys and cables, the load of hay and threw it over to the top of the haystack where stackers (usually two men) would spread it out to make a neat hay stack.

16

The biggest problem with that type of stacker is that occasionally the cable would break and the tines would fall down. Anyone cleaning up under those tines could be hurt or killed. The cable broke twice that summer, but I was quick enough to get out of the way.

3.

When the haying was done, there were fences to mend, corrals to repair, and buildings to get ready for winter. In August we rode up into the mountains to bring the cattle down out of the high country. I got quite good at chasing down strays. Finally, it was the first of September. Al made a deal with the rancher. He would stay on for the winter and help feed the stock. I would go to school.

I still don't know how he got the school to take me into the fourth grade. I looked about the right age, but we had no school records. I guess that little country school didn't stand on formality all that much. We stayed half of the winter. The day school let out for Christmas vacation Al decided we needed to head for warmer weather. We "grabbed a handful of boxcars" and headed south. That means we got on a freight train.

Before school was out for the summer I attended school in three different states. We went where the work was, or where Al's wanderlust took us. If I remember correctly, there were a total of five schools that saw my "smiling face" the first year I was "on the run".

The minute school let out, and I got my report card, we were "on the road". I don't know if they still do it, but in those days there was a convention, of sorts, of Hobos. I don't remember exactly where it took place, but I do remember that the woods were full of people. There must have been four or five hundred camps scattered about. I wandered from one camp to another in total awe. Men sang together, drank beer, and talked about their experiences during the year.

Rails, Gondola, and Boxcar may have been there, but, much to my disappointment, I did not find them. I remember counting the number of people named "Boxcar" after I heard it a few times. I got up to twenty-six before I quit. Most "Boxcars" had another name as well. The most popular Hobo seemed to be Boxcar Benny. Everyone seemed to like him, and followed his leadership. I believe he was some type of Hobo leader. Years later, when I heard about "Hobo Kings" I wondered if he was not the current King, at the time.

In my wandering from camp to camp I was always welcomed. I met men who could not read or write and I met others who claimed to have a Doctorate Degree. One was a medical doctor. He helped those who were sick, or injured. When I visited him he put me to work as his "assistant". I held an old man's hand until he died. I asked, "Why did he die?"

The doctor said, and I never forgot, "He died because it was his time. Death is nothing more than part of living. To die is not as bad as people think".

We helped a man who had nearly cut off his arm. Everyone expected him to bleed to death, but the doctor saved his life. He said, "It was not his time". I don't remember any transfusion, or even anesthesia when the arm was sewed back together. Every day, for a week, I attended to that man's needs.

There were a few women in the camp. They would hug me nearly every time they saw me. Some gave me little treat, like candy. Often, I saw tears in their eyes. I remember asking one woman why she was crying. She sat me down and told me about herself. Her husband and children were killed in a bad automobile accident some three years earlier and she had just gone to pieces, she said she just didn't care any more.

That was the summer of learning, for a ten-year-old boy. Without exception everyone at the camp treated me, not like a kid, but a short adult. They encouraged me to get an education. I remember one very large man. He must have been nearly six-and-a-half-feet tall, and had massive shoulders. His face was hidden behind a great black beard, but what I could see was frightening. His nose was bulbous and pock marked. There was a knife scar that went from his forehead, over one eye, and onto his cheek. I was running past him one day. He reached out and caught me in mid stride, stopping me as though I had hit a brick wall. He held me up in the air with one hand and said, "I don't want you to be here forever. You get educated and get smart. Then when you go into the Army they'll make you an officer and we'll all be proud of you." He laughed with a roar, as he put me down to run off.

I asked Al, "Who was that man?"

Al replied, "That's `Steam Engine'. If he ever hits you, you'll think you have been run over by one. He used to be a prizefighter, but I understand he killed a guy in the ring. I've been told that he tried to join the Army during the war, but they wouldn't take him because he was too big.

The Hobo convention lasted over a month. Al and I stayed the whole time, while most of them moved on as others arrived. I learned how to make campfires, lean-tos, a bed of leaves and branches, and I learned how "Hobo Stew" was made.

I have read many recipes for "hobo stew" over the years. The truth of the matter is that it is the easiest thing in the world to make, but it can't be made in a kitchen. The genuine recipe is simple. You get about a five gallon can with either an open top, or you open it. A lot of restaurants used to throw lard cans out. They are the best. After you wash the can you fill it full of water and boil it real hard over the campfire. After a few minutes you dump the water and refill the can, to a little over two thirds full. Then you dump in what you have. Everyone contributes, and everything is cleaned, and cut into pieces. There are potatoes, carrots, a little asparagus, beets, wild onions, beans, rutabagas, turnips, - anything anyone can contribute. Whatever meat someone brings is dropped in, a rabbit, a grouse or quail, maybe a little roast beef or lamb. This mixture boils away all day. Water is added as needed and whoever wants to eat does so, whenever they have a notion. The stew changes flavor as the day progresses and other ingredients are added from time to time. A good Hobo Stew can be kept going for weeks.

I learned that the "Knights of the Road", as some have called them, had a definite creed. No one breaks the law. One "Bo" never lies to another. Hobos don't take handouts, except from one another. They work for everything they get. They don't pry into another Hobo's affairs, unless invited. They always share what they have, and take care of one another. Any Hobo that could not adhere to the creed was cast out. I heard stories about maverick Hobos being thrown, literally, off a moving train that had other Hobos aboard. No Hobo would have anything to do with them, and the word spread rapidly.

Toward the end of the big "convention" a new man came into the camp. Even I could tell there was something different about him. He was either new to the road, or not a Hobo.

He was there for a couple days when, late one afternoon, the police arrived. There had been a squad car, or two, stop occasionally just to check up on things. This time there were five cars and over a dozen officers. Some of the Hobos gathered around and Boxcar Benny walked up to the officers with his arms up to about his shoulders. The officer in charge said he had orders to search the camp. After some discussion he said they were looking for a man who had raped a little girl in a town thirty, or so, miles to the east. Benny asked if they had any kind of description. Once he was told, he motioned to two of the other "Bo's". They hurried away. A couple minutes later the big, bearded, man called "Steam Engine" came forward dragging the new man. He raised the man into the air and threw him a good ten feet. He landed at the feet of the police officer. The big, booming, voice of Steam Engine said, "Here's your man officer. If he don't give you a full confession, call me."

The Hobo convention broke up a couple days later, and everyone went on to whatever adventure was in store for them. Al and I went back to "working the farms, and ranches".

That was the year that I became a sheepherder. My job was to hang around the flock to keep coyotes away and make sure the sheep didn't get into a field where they didn't belong. Al worked the haying season there, and at some of the neighboring ranches. In late August we worked with the sheep shearers. Sheep ranchers from several ranches would bring their flocks to a central location, for shearing, so there were thousands of sheep to "give a hair cut".

At first I was a "tromper". After the wool had been removed a person would tie it into a bundle and toss it up to me. I was inside of a large sack and would tromp on the wool to pack It into the sack. They decided I was too light for that job. They were not getting enough wool in each big sack. They made me a "penner". All of the sheep were in a big corral. Each shearer had a small pen beside him that held about six or eight sheep. When he finished with one animal he would reach into the pen and drag another one out. I had to keep those little pens full. In the end I graduated to "tier". After the shearer had finished shearing the sheep I would tie the wool into a bundle and toss it up to the tromper. My hands were quick, so I was very good at tying. That last job paid a lot more than being a "penner". Al had been tying wool throughout the whole time.

When school started for the year we were both "loaded with money", so we rented a little house. Al did odd jobs around town while I went to school. I had a job chopping wood after school.

I was the "troupe scribe" for the local Boy Scout troop. My articles were printed in the local newspaper every week. That newspaper consisted of three or four mimeographed sheets of letter size paper, but I was published. When winter made it known that it was there to stay Al was ready to move south again.

I quit trying to keep track of the number of schools I attended. I was either way ahead of the rest of the class, and bored, or I was way behind and working hard to catch up.

Every time I enrolled in a new school the school tough guy would pick a fight. It was similar to the fights animals have, to establish leadership. Sometimes I won. Sometimes I lost. It didn't make any difference. I got to the point that when I entered a new school I would look for the resident bully. My standard challenge was to walk up to him and say, "Hi., I'm the new kid in school. If you feel you have to fight me, let's get it done now". This worked pretty good. They usually backed off and left me alone. Once the other kid said, "OK." and proceeded to beat me up.

4.

In the spring I turned eleven, we rode the rails to Montana and then to Wyoming, where we got jobs on a horse ranch. I learned how to handle a horse in such a way as to teach him to carry a rider. The rancher didn't believe in "breaking" horses. He claimed that he could not ride a bucking horse, but there was not a horse living that he could not teach to be a good saddle horse. We had the same first name and he treated me more like a son than a hired hand. Whenever he went somewhere, he took me along.

One time he took me to another ranch. There was a horse there that the owner claimed was unbreakable. When we arrived, the horse was in the corral and a cowboy was trying to ride it. As we watched they "eared it down" and the cowboy climbed aboard. "Earring an animal down" is simple. One man bites the animal's ear while another mounts it. The poor horse is so concerned about the pain in his ear that he ignores the other discomfort. The cowboy didn't last two jumps. We could see the horse tremble in fright. His eyes showed shear terror and he sweated as though they had been trying to tame him for a long time. When the cowboy got off the ground he grabbed a quirt (a small leather whip) and started beating the horse.

That was all my rancher friend could stand. He jerked the quirt away from the cowboy and told him to get the "hell" out of there. That was the only time I ever saw George mad. Everyone around the corral said that the horse was an "outlaw" and could not be ridden. George told everyone to go back to work and leave us alone. He said, "The kid and I will handle the horse, you men get out of our way and find something else to do besides abusing an animal". I learned, very quickly, that we were there because of a bet.

During the next two hours I saw my hero calm the horse down and saw it learn to trust the man that was working with it. An hour later he was ready to ride. He didn't ride that animal. He put ME on it. I rode him around the corral and then around the ranch's yard. It followed me without any trouble when I let it into the horse trailer we had brought along. I don't know the terms of the bet, but the rancher got the horse, a big wad of money, and I got a forty dollar bonus. All the other rancher, and his friends got, was embarrassed that a kid was riding a horse they could not break, that was an "outlaw".

By the first of August I had trained three horses that had never carried a saddle. They let me ride them, but they did get a little skittish when a full-grown man climbed aboard.

I started school there and rode a horse the three miles to school every day. After six weeks, Al was ready to move on.

We were in town when Al made his decision. I must say, he was a man of action. Before I could think about it we were on a freight headed north. Fortunately, for me, it slowed down and stopped on a siding to wait for a southbound freight on the main line. I remembered my army blanket, and my twenty-two rifle. The blanket was important to me and the rifle had supplied us with meat a lot of times when we would have gone hungry. Al wasn't about to go back, so he said to meet him at a

Hobo camp we knew about near Laurel Montana. I hopped the southbound, and dropped off near the ranch.

I told the rancher, George, that Al had suddenly decided to leave and asked if I could have the blanket and rifle. His wife helped me get all of my things together and packed them neatly in an old suitcase. Al's stuff was dumped in a gunnysack. He even paid me the wages we had coming, but he said not to give any of it to Al. I told him I was sorry to leave, but I had to stay with Al.

As he drove me to town the next day he said, "Your brother has itchy feet boy. Don't you grow up to be like him. I know it is a great adventure for you at this time, but he'll never amount to a hill of beans. When you decide you want a home, come back here". He paid for a ticket on a passenger train. It was strange, sitting in a comfortable chair as the scenery went by, but I didn't see much of it. I cried almost all the way to Laurel. Al and I arrived on the same day.

We didn't stay in Montana. We went south and continued another year of numerous schools, towns, and states. That was the winter that I began to get the idea that Al was tiring of the "brother act". Several times I was left with acquaintances while Al took off for a week or two. I was becoming much more independent and reliable. I guessed that Al figured he had done his job.

I didn't fully catch on until the next spring. We went to another big Hobo Convention for about a month. Al took off, without a word, and was gone most of that time. There was plenty to occupy me. I saw some people I knew and a number of people I did not recognize spoke to me. I went hunting several times and brought back game, so I was always welcome at every fire.

When Al returned, he had a deal for us. We were to join a "Combining Crew" in Oklahoma and follow the wheat harvest all the way north to Canada. While the men were harvesting the wheat I was a roustabout, water boy, errand boy, and I helped with repairs to the equipment. The law said that I had to be fourteen, because I worked with my brother on the crew. Otherwise I had to be eighteen. We lied just like we lied the past two years. I was fourteen when I was ten, eleven, twelve, and even thirteen. After all I had been taught about honesty by the Wrights, and the hobo people, it did not feel right to lie about my age. A man does have to eat. I never knew my true age anyway.

When the crew was not working because of weather, or because they were moving to the next location, I became part of the "advance team". There were three of us. Our job was to line up crops for harvest. The other two were the salesmen. I was the "go-for" and cook. We camped out at night, so it was my job to set up camp, cook, and clean up. They dropped me, and the camping gear, at the camp location and then went off to find accounts.

Al claimed that we would really make good money. He said we'd be "set up for the winter" and we would stay in one place. At the end of summer we were in North Dakota right next to the Canadian Border. I was afraid that if I went into Canada they would not let me come back, or they would find out who I was and send me back to Texas and an orphan's home. The vast amount of money Al thought we would have turned out to be a lot less. When they paid me, during the season, I saved almost everything, but Al spent most of his earnings.

We grabbed a "handful of boxcars" meaning to head south, but caught a wrong train and wound up in

Ekalaka Montana. We were hanging around town, not doing much, when I landed a position taking care of an elderly lady who had broken her hip. She was getting around, but it was the second time that she had broken the same hip in less than a year. Her family wanted someone to help her around the house and just be there in case something else happened. I got settled in and Al took off.

The woman was in her late eighties, but she was tough. She told me stories about Norway while we sat and ate "lefsa". I had all the money I needed for school clothes and incidental spending so I refused the ten dollars a month the family had agreed to pay me. Al got some of my summer's savings, but he did not know about most of it. I had my own room, meals, and a good companion. We became very close. I was treated more like a member of her family every day. In fact she started referring to me as her grandson.

Good things never lasted forever, for me. Not long before Christmas vacation her son visited. He asked me if I wouldn't like to be with my own family over the holidays. I took the hint. I was out of there as soon as vacation started. It was the first time I rode the rails by myself, but I was an accomplished traveler by then. By the time I got to Oklahoma I was very concerned about school. I located a vacant shack, on the outskirts of a small town, and moved in. It was so run down that I thought no one would mind, and might not notice. If I was run off before school was out for the summer, I would just move to another school, another town, another state.

When I left the old lady, she gave me an old duffle bag and helped me pack. I had not opened that bag, so I was quite surprised when I finally opened it and found an envelope with over a hundred dollars in it.

The note said "Merry Christmas" and was signed "Grandma". I was in the shack only two days before school started again.

I went to the school and told them that my dad and I had just moved to town. I said that my dad had to work, so he sent me to get registered. I guess I had learned to be a pretty good con artist. They believed me, and sent for my records. It was nearly two weeks before the owner of the shack came by, to see why smoke was coming out of the chimney. I knew immediately who that old man was, but he didn't let on at all. He came up to me while I was doing some repair work on the door. He was very friendly, as though he was a neighbor. He helped me with the door and then I invited him in. We sat and talked about all the things I had done to improve the shack, about my schoolwork, my grades, and etc. He asked if I liked school so I told him, "A man has to have an education". It was nearly an hour before he changed the subject back to the building. He said I had done a good job making the shack livable and then casually mentioned that he owned the place.

I remember looking at that old man's eyes and deciding not to lie, but to tell him as little truth as necessary. I told him about the old lady, and my blatant invitation to leave. I pointed out that I had actually improved his property and asked if I could stay. I even offered to pay a little rent. Instead, he offered me a deal. I was to live with him and do chores for my board and room. I thought it was amazing that I went through the entire seventh grade in only two schools.

5.

The minute school was out for the summer I took off. Too many people were asking too many questions about the father I had invented. The old man knew I was an orphan and, if asked, would say as much, but he would not volunteer the information. The old specter of the orphans home was once again to influence my life. I went all the way north and lived with the Blackfeet Indians.

I was hanging out in a restaurant, in Browning Montana, when I was distracted by the antics of another boy about my age. He was flirting with the waitress. I went over and sat down at the counter, next to him. I said, "Hey man, that's my girl you're after". He allowed that it was him she loved and not me, so we asked her to choose which one she loved. She reached over the counter and put one hand on his cheek and the other on mine. "I love you both. Now get out of here and make room for paying customers."

The boy was a Blackfeet Indian named, (of all things) Alfred Newman. We became fast friends that day. He was the first friend, of my own age, that I ever had. We had very little in common, but there was a chemistry between us that is impossible to describe. Toward evening, after wandering around all day, he found out that I didn't have a place to stay. He invited me to spend the night with him. His parents said they didn't mind as long as he got his work done. I asked if I could work too, and was informed

31

that everyone who eats at their house works. My overnight stay lasted a month.

We did the morning chores, milking cows, slopping hogs, and etc. The girls of the family fed the chickens and gathered eggs. Some times we cleaned barns or helped in the fields, but we had plenty of time for relaxation. We spent hours swimming, fishing, and riding horses. During one of our horse back excursions I met a religious group called Hutterites.

The Hutterites didn't believe in many of the modern conveniences. They all wore the same clothes and lived in a commune. They offered me a job when I told them that I had herded sheep. I started my new job the very next week. I lived in a little trailer, out where the flock was grazing. Twice each day a girl would drive a wagon out to my trailer with generous amounts of food. I was never told her name, and we never had a conversation, but we began to look forward to seeing one another.

The trailer was moved to new pasture two different times. By the time I arrived with the sheep there was always a meal waiting for me, and a girl, who would smile when no one was looking at us. When fall arrived, and I got ready to find a school, I learned that they were generous with their money as well as their food. I left with the most money I had ever seen at one time, nearly eight hundred dollars.

Al and I had spent a few days in a cabin a few miles south of the little town of Absarokee, Montana, the first summer we were together. I decided to find it again. I didn't have any problem finding the town. All I had to do was drop off the train at Columbus and hitchhike about thirty miles straight south. Once in town I stopped at a hardware store to buy a carton of shells for my rifle.

I met a guy, a couple years older than me, at the store. We hit it off very well and when he got off work a few minutes later we "hung out" together for a while. We discovered that we were in the same grade. He said he had been sick for a long time and missed a lot of school. I described the log cabin where I intended to live. He said, "Sounds like the Bennett place". Then he proceeded to tell me where it was, and how to get there. He wanted to take me, but his dad wouldn't let him.

I took the road out of town and caught a ride most of the way. My ride needed to go straight ahead at the only paved fork in the road. I walked the last mile. Ronnie, the guy at the hardware store, was right. The place I was looking for was the "Bennett place".

The cabin sat a good quarter mile off the road, beside a stream. It was surrounded by trees on the edge of a meadow. There was the cabin, a barn, and a spring of sweet water. It was just as I remembered, and expected; also, it was vacant. I moved in. A few days later I went into town to register for school, buy food, and see if I could find the owner of my cabin.

Keeping people from becoming inquisitive had become an art form, for me. This time my dad was working out of town and would only be able to visit once a month. My mom was very ill and could not come to town, or receive visitors. They bought it! I was registered in school. When asked about my dad's profession I told them he worked with the railroad, but I didn't know exactly what he did. I just knew he traveled a lot. I couldn't tell anyone my mother's problem either, because my parents had not confided in me.

My new friend, Ronnie, was getting off work and offered to drive me home, so I loaded up with groceries. His dad was out of town that day so his mother gave permission. I learned that Mr. Bennett, the

33

owner of the cabin, was on an extended vacation and no one seemed to know when he would return. I left messages at two different locations, the grocery store and the bar.

Ronnie became my new "best friend". He spent a lot of time with me. I soon learned why. He had no other friends. The other kids in our class rejected him because he was older and a whole lot smarter. Kids his own age didn't have anything in common with him. We studied together and even went into partnerships in a business venture, for a while.

Ronnie would rent his step-dad's truck and we would haul garbage for people. We picked up every week and charged five dollars a can, by the month. We were doing quite well until someone teased Ronnie's step-dad about having a garbage collector for a son. By then the snow was making the roads slick. So we didn't argue much when the truck rental deal was canceled.

I started a trap line with some traps I had found in the barn. I was catching rabbits, weasel, muskrats, and skunks. There was a hide dealer in town that paid me a little less than he could get for them in the city. Skunk pelts brought two and a half dollars each. Most of my pelts were skunk. One day I wore the wrong overshoes to school. When those overshoes warmed up, smelling of skunk, I got kicked out for the rest of the day. They almost dismissed the whole school.

I had several ways to make money. I never really cared about eating trout, but I loved catching them. Once a week I sold one mess of fish to a farmer about a half-mile down the road, and a much bigger mess to the local butcher. Every now and then the butcher asked me to get him a deer. He would give me fifty dollars each time.

My method of fishing was different. I netted, snared, grappled, and shot them. I even tried catching them with a fishing pole now and then. Snaring was easy. I made a loop out of a copper wire, tied it on to the end of a willow pole and slipped the noose over the fish. When the wire was just behind his front fins, I jerked him out. Grappling is different. I would reach under the brush in the stream, where the fish were hiding, or under rocks. Then I would slowly slide my hand around the girth and squeeze. The only way you can shoot a fish is to catch him in fairly shallow water, say a foot deep. You don't hit it, you knock it out with the concussion of the bullet hitting the water. It floats to the surface and you grab it. If you are not quick enough the fish will recover and swim away.

As usual, I was not popular in the school so I didn't care to go out at recess time. I got teased and then I got in fights. When the teacher started insisting that I go out, I started doing things that would call for staying in during recess as punishment. They were reluctant to keep me after school because I was riding the school bus, and because of my mother's ailment. One day the butcher's daughter offered to pay me to do her math during recess. I had found yet another way to make money. This started a good business. Before long I had several "clients". I guess they went home and copied the work. No one ever said anything about all those people having the same handwriting. I know the teacher knew what I was doing. I don't remember being happy, or sad, about my life in that environment. I had never been either happy or sad about my life. As I look back I believe it was the first time I was truly content since I left home.

I got past Thanksgiving all right, but as Christmas approached I began my usual period of depression much earlier. The difference that made this Christmas so important to me was that I had something to share, and no one with which to share.

I was living in a winter wonderland. Clean, unbroken, snow in the meadows led to thousands of trees; every branch laden with ice and snow. At night the light of the moon made the snow glisten as if it were glowing, against the blackness of the forest. During the day the branches reflected the winter sun in every color of the rainbow, as though they all had been decorated with lights for the Holiday. Wild animals and birds could be seen almost at any time. I really felt that I needed to share all of it. Circumstances took care of that problem for me.

I stayed in town after school one Friday evening and went to the movies with Ronnie. It was after ten o'clock at night when he dropped me off at the gate. We didn't think he would make it into the cabin without getting stuck. I began walking to the house. I was surprised to see truck tracks leading to the place. When I arrived, I saw a four-wheel drive truck by the front door and all of my lamps lit. I didn't have electricity so I used kerosene lamps. They even had a fire in both stoves. From the sparks coming out of the chimney, I knew they had too much fire in the pot-bellied heater.

I approached the door with mixed emotions. I no longer felt the cold. I was angry that someone was in "my house" burning my kerosene, and the wood that I had cut. I was scared that I was in trouble for living there without permission. I was apprehensive about my immediate future. I was confused about how I was going to handle the situation.

As I came up to the kitchen door, a boy about two years older than me opened the door and came outside. I said, "What's going on here?"

He looked at me, "We're moving in. Who are you?"

"My name is George", I replied, "I live here".

He looked confused. "Well we live here now. The landlord's inside and he rented this house to my mom."

I walked into the kitchen. One man, a woman, and two girls were busy putting things in various cupboards and chests of drawers. There were cardboard boxes scattered all over the room.

One of the girls squealed, then said, "Mom, who's that."

I ignored everyone but the man. "Sir, are you the landlord? I need to talk to you."

He acknowledged that he was, indeed, the owner of the property and told me that he thought it would be better if he talked to my parents. Obviously, he knew he was talking to the "squatter" who was using his property.

I said, "Please sir, can we sit down and talk?" I gave my best smile and gestured toward the kitchen table. Then I looked at the woman. "I see you found my can of coffee. Could we have a cup please?"

We discussed the situation. When I explained that I was not a "squatter" and had tried to get word to him his initial hostility vanished. Mr. Bennett was sympathetic when I confessed that I was alone in the world and only wanted to go to school and be left alone. I did spin a good yarn about how my parents were dead and my brother had taken care of me, but we had a falling out and he had left me to fend for myself. After a long discussion we came to an understanding. I would continue to live there and so would the woman and her kids.

I insisted on paying my own way. The lady, Mrs. "E", had very little income and three kids to support. I only called her Mrs. E because her last name was so hard to pronounce. Mr. Bennett told me he had agreed to rent the cabin to Mrs. E for ten dollars a month. I went over to my bed and pulled a loose piece of chinking from between the logs just above where my head would rest. I took my stash of money and paid Mr. Bennett a hundred and twenty dollars. He gave me a receipt that showed the rent paid from the time I first moved in until September of the following year. Not only did I pay the rent I agreed to furnish all the meat the family could eat. I contributed the food that I already had in the house to the "community pot".

The cabin had only two rooms, but one of them was very large. The large central room was the kitchen, living, and dining area. The other room was a large bedroom. We moved things around and made two rooms at one end of the large room. Mr. Bennett, later, made partitions, so the girls could have more privacy. Mrs. E took over my bedroom. I contributed some of the money to buy two sets of double deck bunk beds for the two new bedrooms.

The two girls were "Mary", about 17, and "Alice", about 14. The boy, "Billy", was sixteen. Mary and Billy had quit school after the eighth grade. Billy took over the project of getting wood for the fires. This increased my free time for studies and hunting.

Christmas came with a rush. School let out for vacation and I went shopping the same day. It was the first time I had celebrated that holiday since leaving home. Although I bought presents for the family, and tried to get in the "Christmas Spirit", the depression I always felt was more acute than ever. Part of that may have been from my disappointment when I took my "new family" out to show them my "winter wonderland". All they saw was the snow, ice, and cold.

Christmas day was particularly hard. I didn't feel bad about the dinner. My twenty-two had provided the Pheasants, and the Venison. After the meal I retreated to the barn to work on stretching some hides. It was well after dark when I returned to the house.

All during the season, and especially on Christmas day they tried to make me feel their joyous mood. It was nothing they, or anyone, did that made me feel so sad. It was the realization that they had something I had never really had: they were family.

Realizing why I have depression on Christmas, Thanksgiving, and Mother's Day has only helped me cope. It has never lessened. Now that I have my own family, Thanksgiving and Christmas have been a whole lot better, but old habits die hard. Old hurts die even harder.

Between Christmas and New Years I took Billy out and showed him my trap line. When the week was gone he knew it well. I turned my trapping enterprise over to him. My "tutoring" business was expanding and I needed more time. Besides, Billy had not been able to find work and he felt he needed "to contribute to the family". Mary had a job as a waitress at the cafe in town. I never saw either of them give their mother money to help with the expenses. Alice was attending high school. We walked to the bus stop together. I was surprised one morning when she stopped about half way to the road and commented about how pretty the trees were, when the branches were laden with snow.

The first Saturday, after school started again, I had to go into town to collect the remainder of my hide money. Billy came with me, so he could meet the fur buyer. Billy decided to stay in town for a while, so I started hitchhiking home. My only coat smelled of skunk so I never wore it to school, or into town. After the overshoe incident, I didn't dare. A rancher that lived about five miles past the cabin picked me up just outside of town. They had a son who was in my class at school. Everyone called him Og and I thought the name came from his initials, but it didn't. That was actually his name. He was not one of the gang that picked on me and beat on me every chance they had. He was not a friend either. In fact I don't think he ever even spoke to me, before or after that one day.

We were in the back seat of his parent's car. He looked over at me after we had gone about two miles and said, "I got a new coat for Christmas. I want you to have my old one". Then he asked his mother if he could give it to me. They drove me to their ranch, to get the coat, and then back to the driveway into my house. To my amazement not one person in the whole school said a word about me wearing Og's old coat. A lot of kids even started leaving me alone. I still didn't have any friends, other than Ronnie, but I had a lot fewer active enemies.

The first thing I did, after getting that coat, was to catch the worst cold I had ever had in my life, but it got cured in a unique way. A couple weeks later I was out hunting and happened to come across an old shack. There was a dead man in there. I had heard about the man. He was from somewhere in the south, and made his living bootlegging. Buying liquor was legal enough, but he sold it after the liquor stores were closed for the night. He was well known in the area. I looked around for a while and located his still. I confiscated two bottles of moonshine before leaving to report my find. The County Sheriff came out with the County Coroner and recovered the body, but they never found the still.

I would take a sip of moonshine every morning before going to school. I never caught another cold, but I probably gained a reputation with that liquor on my breath every day. One day Billy caught me taking my morning sip. That night, after school, I told him about the still and all the bottles of booze that were stored there. He brought all the whiskey down to the barn. His mother never knew about his "stash" of "wet goods". He made a lot of money selling it to his friends.

Just about a week before the end of the school year Mrs. E took me to town and helped me pick out a suit for Eighth Grade Graduation. During the ceremony the principal would announce the name of the student, and ask his, or her, parents to stand. When my name was announced no one stood. Finally Mrs. E stood up, but everyone knew she was not my mother. I overheard two of the town's women discussing me and wondering aloud about my family. I had a feeling that some of the people were looking at me differently. Now that I had drawn their attention, I decided I had better get out of the area before they asked too many questions.

I left most of my things with Mrs. E. The only possessions I took were a couple changes of clothes, my blanket and my twenty-two. I left them most of my money, only taking about fifty dollars. Ronnie gave me a ride to the train yards and dropped me off. That was the last time I ever saw him. He left home shortly thereafter and his parents never knew where he had gone.

6.

That summer, after graduating from grade school, was to be my vagabond year. I had almost decided that my school days were over. I traveled all over the Midwest for a full month. I looked for Al at the annual Hobo convention, but I didn't find him, or anyone who knew him.

While there, I met a woman. She looked as though she was over fifty-years-old, but she wasn't. After I had stayed at her campfire for a few minutes she began to cry. Eventually she told me her story.

When the Second World War broke out, she and her husband were in the Army. She was a nurse and her husband was an officer. They had three sons. One was to graduate from high school and the other two had just graduated the previous year. They were twins. The family was stationed in Hawaii, where she was a nurse at the big military hospital. On December fifth she was sent to the Philippines to help bring back a patient for care in Hawaii.

Her husband was killed when the Japanese bombed Pearl Harbor. Shortly hereafter she was taken prisoner. I didn't understand exactly what she meant at the time, but I knew it had to be something very bad. She said, "They abused me nearly every day for over four years".

Her three sons joined the service. One was killed in North Africa. The second died on Normandy beach. Her youngest son was killed on Saipan. She never knew about the fate of her family until the Army liberated her internment camp near the end of the war.

After the war she lived for a short time in a small house in Nebraska. One day a hobo came to her door asking for work in exchange for a meal. She let him mow her lawn and fed him. During the meal they talked. I remember her saying, "He didn't leave for a week and when he did, I went with him".

I tried to console her by repeating what the doctor had told men about death years earlier. She said, "I know, honey, there are things worse than death. In prison camp they tortured me while they were doing things to me that you are too young to know. She showed me where they had pulled out some of her fingernails. I saw the round scars where they had burned her with cigarettes. She said they were all over her body. She said, "Yes death is not so bad. There are times when it can be a blessing".

She was not the first, and certainly not the last, to give me many lessons on what it means to be an American. Her story was the most effective. She said, "You are an American, be proud of that and be like my husband and sons. They fought to defeat the animals that did these things to me. Stay in school and get a good education. Whenever this country is in trouble, you fight for her. Our country isn't perfect but it's a whole lot better than anything else".

That night the lady came over to my camp. She drew me aside and said she had decided to go home. For some reason she thanked me and then give me a piece of paper with her name and address written on it. She said that when I decided I wanted to, I could come live with her, and she would take good care of me. That could be exactly what should have happened, but I was still full of adventure. I hung on to that address for a long time, but, like a lot of things, it got lost.

7.

I left the camp. It had lost its appeal. I wound up in Wyoming, not far from Yellowstone Park. I had learned that the best way to find a job in a small town was at the local restaurant, or the bar. I made it known that I was looking at the cafe, first, and then went over to the bar. The bartender didn't like the idea of me being there, but when all I ordered was a bottle of soda pop, he got friendlier. After he asked me why I was there, and I answered, he called to a man who had just come in, "Hey Fred, didn't you say you needed a hunter? This kid might be able to help you".

Fred and I talked for a while. After I convinced him that I could handle the job, in spite of my youth, he decided to take me out to his ranch and see if I could shoot. I told him that when I pointed my twenty-two at something, I hit it. On the way out to his place he filled me in on the problem.

There were five or six big sheep ranchers in the area who used the high mountain meadows for summer grass. The small outfits, and even the larger ones, had run most of the coyotes out of the low country, so they had a major problem with them killing sheep during the time the flocks were in the high country. The herders were doing what they could, but they had to stay with the flock. The Sheep Rancher's Association had given Fred the job of securing a free-roaming hunter, with a good "eye". The main trouble he had encountered in finding such a man was that no one wanted to spend all that time alone. Those who were willing couldn't shoot.

He said that, if I could hit his target, I would have a job until they brought the sheep down, in the fall. It would pay two hundred dollars, plus a twelve dollar bounty on every set of coyote ears I brought in. I said I'd take the job. He said, "We'll see".

Once we arrived at the ranch he handed me a 220 Swift rifle. He said, "Practice with this for a while. You'll find it a little different than a twenty-two". The rifle shoots a twenty-two slug, but has a lot of gunpowder behind it. This one was equipped with a powerful scope. I discovered that I could see targets a lot further away than normal, and that the bullet had almost zero drop, even at two hundred yards. After about thirty shots I felt comfortable with the weapon.

At dusk, Fred set up a silhouette of a coyote about two hundred yards away, and ordered me to kill it. After I fired the third shot he went out and picked up the target. When he came back, he said, "Not bad kid. Let's see how you do in the morning". I noticed three holes in the target about where I had figured the heart would be located.

Very early the next morning we did the target test again. When he picked up the target, he didn't say a word, but he had a slight smile. During breakfast he asked me a lot of questions about camping, cooking over a campfire, and horses. By eight in the morning a saddle horse and a packhorse were waiting for me.

We loaded the horses and their gear into a trailer and headed toward the foothills. We talked during the ride. I had a feeling he wasn't too sure about hiring someone so young for this job. I made it a point to assure him that I would do my best and give him a day's work, for a day's pay. I listened intently as he told me about coyotes, and how they liked to hunt late in the evening and in early morning. He said I would be wise to hunt during the night, when the moon was bright. He gave me a quota. "I want fifteen sets of ears before fall".

The dirt road we followed led to the lower one of the sheepherder's camps. There were three others, one further up in the mountains, one to the north, and one to the south. He said I was to keep in touch and make sure I talked to at least one of the herders every week. He cautioned me not to shoot one of their dogs by mistake. I arrived at the "High" camp about mid-afternoon, where, as instructed, I spent the rest of the day and the night. I learned where most of the sheep had been killed, and where coyotes had been seen. I listened to a great deal of advice. The next morning I was on my way. By noon I was about where I wanted to set up my base camp. I planned to make excursions out from there. With the information I had gathered, and the topographical maps Fred gave me I felt I was centrally located. I spent the rest of the day setting up the tent, a fire pit and a latrine.

I took short trips by foot and longer ones by horseback. The first day I got three coyotes as they fought over a fresh kill. I killed at least one, and generally more, a day for the first three weeks. Three different times I never even had to leave camp to get a kill. Coyotes are curious. They came to look me over and I spotted one now and again. I hung the ears out to dry on a branch. In twenty-one days I had thirty-three "scalps" drying on several branches. I didn't see another one of the animals for a solid week.

Fred had gotten reports from the various herders I had contacted. After that dry week, he met me at the same herder's camp where I had last seen him. He said I had done a better job than he expected. We discussed the situation and he decided that there would be no more trouble with coyotes during the rest of the season. He took me into town and paid me off. He had an argument about the amount of money with some of the other ranchers, but he saw that I collected everything that was coming to me.

I decided to go back to the cabin near Absarokee. I got to the cabin just two weeks before Labor Day, and the start of school. Much to my disappointment, Mrs. E and her kids were still living there. They welcomed me as an old friend, or even as a member of the family, yet. I had counted on being alone for the winter.

Alice asked me if I had all of my school clothes. That was when I made the mistake of telling her that I had absolutely no intention of continuing my education. I informed her that I had gone to school only because the law said I had to go, but school had never been fun for me because of the other students. I said I was through being teased by rich kids.

8.

Alice told her brother Billy about my decision. Billy took me out to the barn and informed me that I had a choice. I could go to high school, or I could have him "beat-up on me every day". I was five feet, four inches at the time and he was six feet, one inch. I was skinny. He was husky. I decided to go to school. I realized that I could have just left, but I needed an excuse to continue going to school. The admonition of my female Hobo friend and others had not been entirely forgotten. I never realized this until years later. The next day Alice took me into town and helped me buy school clothes. Then she started to, "civilize" me.

That was the first time I ever owned, or wore, under shorts, or tee shirts. She got my hair cut and bought me a comb. My hair hadn't been combed over a half dozen times since I ran away from the Wrights. Alice changed me from a wild thing, to a human. It didn't help a lot, as far as the way other kids treated me, but I felt a lot better about myself. I even started brushing my teeth on a regular basis.

About two weeks after starting high school I found that I liked it. I could progress more rapidly and the classes were less boring. I went to the Principal and talked to him about other courses. After I told him I was interested in Business Law, He showed me a catalogue of correspondence courses that were available to high school students. It took about two weeks for the complete course to arrive. My progress was such that in another week we ordered another course. The Business Law course was finished before the new one arrived. I was able to keep up with my regular classes and even had a job tutoring the Principal's daughter in math. By Christmas break I was taking a minimum of three correspondence courses at a time. I didn't have a social life, and very few chores. I paid for my room and board by paying the rent with my summer money and used my twenty-two to provide meat for the table.

Three days into the holiday I learned that the County Sheriff had been asked to pick me up. Some of the "Church Ladies" thought I should be in an approved foster home. I was out of town fast, but not before visiting my Principal.

I explained that "I had to return home because my mother was very ill", but I wanted to continue with the correspondence courses in which I was currently enrolled. He gave me all of the material and said to send him the tests. He would see that I got proper credit. He even gave me self-addressed envelopes and one of the catalogues that showed the courses available. He wrote a letter and sealed it. He said I was to give it to the Principal of my next school. His next words told me that he knew a lot more about me than I had told him.

He said, "Whenever you change schools, always take this letter with you and give it to your new Principal. He will help you. If you ever have any trouble, write to me."

By New Years day I was in a small town in Oklahoma by the name of Elk City. I met a family there who were suppliers of Rodeo stock. They gave me a job helping with the livestock while I attended school. I found that I was way ahead of my class in every subject because the previous school had progressed further. I checked in with the Principal and gave him the letter. Before long I was totally engrossed in my studies.

When my boss saw what I was doing he refused to let me work. He said I needed all of my time for my education. This fortuitous arrangement lasted until spring break.

One day my boss called me into his office. It was time for them to start moving stock for the Rodeo season and they needed to close the ranch for a while. I would have to find another place to live. He said he had a friend in Montana that he thought could put me up, if I agreed to work for him.

Arrangements were made with the rancher in Montana, and the school I was attending. My extra courses were to go with me. A week's vacation for spring break gave me the opportunity to move. The break for the two schools didn't coincide so I was forced to miss a few days. The work at my new place of residence was very easy. It was obvious that this rancher did not really need me. He had two sons of his own, one my age and another a couple years younger. He specialized in Black Angus Bulls, claiming to be the "biggest bull shipper in the state".

I had not been in the new school three weeks when the Principal called me into his office. He said he had been looking at my school records and wanted to know if I would like to continue my studies during the summer vacation. We had several sessions together. In the end he had me signed up for several courses. He gave me his address and said to send him my workbooks, tests, and papers. As I finished each course he would take care of everything for me. During the wintertime I had always taken the final tests in the Principal's office. Since that was no longer possible the

Principal had my employer's wife certified to administer tests.

It was a summer of hard work on the ranch and much study in my off hours. Other than that, there is one thing that was significant. I happened very soon after the beginning of summer vacation. We had moved the herd from winter pasture up to their "upper ranch" in the mountains for summer graze. Leonard, the owner's eldest son, and I had the job of bringing back the horses that had been used on the trail drive.

In that area of Montana the Rocky Mountains rise abruptly out of low rolling hills. The upper ranch was up a valley formed by a river between two tall mountains. The local people called those mountains the "Tetons", which means woman's breasts in the Indian language. The river was even named "Teton". On the south side of the river, just after leaving the mountains, was an old Indian village. Leonard took me over to see it. I could still see the circles of stones for the Tepees, and where their fires had been. We searched the ground and found numerous beads and arrowheads. I had found Indian beads, and arrowheads, before, but this was much more impressive. I had lived with Indians and had learned much about their culture, their history, and their way of life before the white man came. I believe that the old Indian village solidified my life-long interest in the old Indian Tribes. I began to read every thing I could find about them and talked with elderly Indians at every opportunity. I became an unrecognized expert.

Leonard wanted to leave after spending a couple hours there. I could have stayed for a week, but I needed to go with him.

It was about thirty miles by road from the main ranch to the upper ranch. There were only two or three ranches between the two. Leonard knew where all the gates were located, so we cut across. Our ride would be only about fifteen miles. We were about five miles from our destination when we had our second adventure of the day. We were riding along, away from any roads, when we saw a car stuck in a mud hole that was in the middle of a field. We rode over to see if we could help. Two men were standing beside the car. Leonard asked how they got stuck in the only mud hole for miles. They laughed, in an embarrassed way, and asked if we could help. We handed one of the men the lead ropes for the two horses each of us were leading, and we roped the front bumper, one at each end. The other man got into the vehicle and we used our horses to help the car out of the mud.

The man we left holding the lead ropes introduced himself as A.B. Guthrie Jr. I was flabbergasted. I was shaking hands with a famous author. We knew the book well. It was the one mothers, and schools, forbid children to read. There was a lot of controversy about "The Big Sky" when it first came out. Some parts of the book were quite explicit about the sexual habits of some of the early fur traders, and Indians. Historically, it was accurate, but a lot of people didn't think it should have been put down on paper.

Times do change. At that time, Montana was called "The Treasure State". That is that the word, Montana, was supposed to mean. I think it is because of Mr. Guthrie's book that Montana is now called "The Big Sky Country". That meeting may have impressed me more than I thought, at the time. Today, I am an author. I have admired a man I met only once, and only for a few minutes, over forty years before this writing.

I finished the last of my summer correspondence courses about the first of August. I couldn't get hold of the high school Principal for about three days, so I stayed in town, to wait for him. I had just finished my conference with him when I happened to meet a man who hauled lumber from the northwestern part of the state, to the southwestern part. He said he was making a lot of money buying lumber, hauling it nine hundred miles, and selling it at three times his cost. He hired me to help him.

We made one trip. He paid all of our expenses and gave me one dollar every day, "for spending money". After we had delivered the last of our load I expected to be paid.

He gave me another dollar and informed me that I had been paid all I was going to get. I left him and caught a ride, going west.

I wound up in the town of Three Forks, where I landed a job in a "gypo" sawmill. A "gypo" sawmill is a small, independently owned operation. They usually cut trees on National Forest land. I started as a "limber". After the trees were cut down by the "faller" I had the job of cutting off all off the limbs. After a week I was on the "green chain", which meant that after the two by fours were cut they would come down a conveyer belt and I had to stack them on the truck. We cut one truckload a day. That position lasted a little over two weeks. The law says that, in order to work in the woods, you have to be eighteen. One day the government timber scaler came by. He saw me and asked my age. He didn't believe me when I said I was old enough and demanded that I be let go immediately. The logger had no choice, if he wanted to keep cutting government timber.

During that time, I never had an actual home. I had located myself about a mile out of town, in the woods. It was a place where there were no roads, or houses, nearby. I built a lean-to and was camping out while working with the sawmill. Every morning I would catch a ride to work by meeting some of the men at a cafe where we all went for breakfast. It had been a lean summer and I was nearly broke, so renting a place was out.

Every night, after work, I improved on the camp. I built a second shelter facing the first and then filled in between them. When it rained one day, and there was no work, I gathered grass and mixed it with mud. Then I plastered the outside of my dwelling. It resembled an Indian Hogan. There was a smoke hole in the top and an old horse blanket for a door. Even when the nights started getting colder the place was warm.

My bed was made of pine needles and I used my army blanket for covers. I found a couple old wooden boxes to use as a cupboard and a table. I used the local Laundromat to wash my clothes and my twenty-two to supply meat. Three days before the start of school I went down to the high school and made arrangements. I used my final paycheck from the mill to buy school clothes, a kerosene lamp, and kerosene. I even bought a sleeping bag with an air mattress. The old alarm clock that I had used for years finally broke so I had to get another one. While making that purchase I landed another job.

A man wanted someone to peel fence posts. We agreed on a price, per post, and he promised to pay me for what I did on a daily basis. Since I was starting school, I could only work in the evening and on weekends, but he was in no hurry to get the job done.

He took me to a great pile of cedar posts that were covered with bark. He said he wanted them all clean by spring. The first bunch was easy and I made good wages, but then I got into the ones that had been cut for a long time. It was almost impossible to remove the bark from them. My wages went down considerably and I worked a lot harder. I landed a few jobs cutting firewood for people. It helped my pocketbook.

I brushed my teeth and washed up by going to school early. The janitor would let me in before anyone else arrived. Once that was done I would study until classes started. I got my daily bath after Physical Education classes. I was not able to take all the correspondence courses I wanted, because of work, but I managed to finish four before the Christmas break.

I didn't even try to associate with the other students. I kept to myself and spent every spare moment either studying or working. In spite of that, I seemed to have gained somewhat of a reputation. A rather obnoxious individual tried to pick a fight with me. I look him in the eye and said, "don't even think about it!". Then I turned my back and walked away. I still don't know what was happening behind me, but I heard another kid say, "I don't think I'd do that". My bluff worked. Everyone left me alone.

First semester finals were over by the time I got in trouble. Someone got curious about the smoke from my campfire and the path I had made through the snow. The Sheriff was sent out to find out what was going on in the woods. I was not there when the Sheriff arrived, but I knew he had been there. I followed the tracks his four-wheel drive made and then his footprints to my Hogan. I knew he would be back, so I packed up my things and left town.

9.

I decided I had had enough snow for the year, so I headed south. I wound up in Pinedale Arkansas. For the first week I slept wherever I could find shelter and went to school during the day. I hung out at an out-of-the-way cafe. The owner, Slim, let me wash dishes for meals. One day he offered me a job and agreed to pay me by letting me live in a room in the back of the building, plus a small allowance. I agreed and moved in immediately.

I was able to continue school and take some more extra courses. I took over a back booth and did homework between times when the dishes needed attention. Before long I was waiter, casher, dishwasher, busboy and short order cook.

Business was so slow I still had time to study. There was a bar next to the cafe, with a door between the two. Slim spent most of his time in there and left the cafe for me to run. I opened for him at five thirty every morning and ran the place until time for school. He usually showed up in time to relieve me, but two different times I left the place in the hands of a regular customer and went to school. The customers gave Slim such a hard time that he never did it again.

Spring finally came and school was out for the summer. A week later Slim was forced to close the business. He was drinking all of the profits. He slipped me a hundred dollars the day we locked the doors for good.

I decided I had had all of the south I could stand. I grabbed a handful of boxcars and headed north. Anyone who has ever lived in the south knows what a "cracker" is, or, as it was called in those days, "poor white trash". I never heard the term "cracker" until much later in life. All of the other students treated me as though I was a sub-human, and most of the teachers. I got into many fistfights that winter.

Some of those fights were with knives, or razors. I carry two scars because of that. We were fighting with fists at first, but I began to get the better of my opponent. He pulled out a razor and took a swipe at me. He cut me just above the knees with the first attempt. The razor cut through my jeans and laid open a two inch cut on both legs. I still won the fight, because he took off running when he saw the blood. The school nurse put "butterfly" bandages on the cuts to hold the flesh together. I had difficulty walking for a few days. She said I should go to a doctor and have the cuts sewn, but I never bothered.

The only people I knew who were decent to me were the people around the restaurant and the principal. I was probably an oddity to the principal. It was not often one of his students actually asked for more subjects and more courses. He cooperated fully, but not until he had a copy of my transcript, and the letter that always accompanied me.

A week after I left school, I was in Missoula Montana. I looked around town for a while, while waiting for a freight out that was headed north. While there, I ran into an old friend, Rails. I was walking down the street, when I heard a voice behind me, "Caboose, is that you?" I turned around to see a man I had just passed going the other way. He had turned around and stood in the middle of the sidewalk. I did not recognize him at first. He was clean-shaven and wore a business suit. This man was as clean as Rails had been dirty. I did recognize his lopsided grin though.

We had little chance to talk. I had to catch a train and he had to go to work, but we took the time for a cup of coffee in a nearby restaurant. When I inquired about his new life, he said, "Oh, I met a woman and decided to go back to work". When I asked what he did for a living I did not expect to hear what he said. "I'm a professor of Economics at the University of Montana". I've always wished I had accepted his invitation to stay with him, and his family, for a few days. What a story he must have had to tell.

That was the summer that an acquaintance had gotten me a job working as a section hand. One of the men I met, while riding the rails, said he was a section hand on the Great Northern Railroad. He was a man who loved to talk, so I listened to his stories, and he had a lot of them. His name was, "Mack". He was of Irish stock, not that he had any sign of an accent, but he did have the red hair. His beard was so tough that, when he shaved, he had to use an old fashioned straight razor. He usually waited until his beard was long, and his wife made him shave. I once took a strand of that hair and twisted it into a loop like it was copper wire.

He said they would be hiring some extra help for the summer and he could get me hired. I said I'd be there. When I showed up at his place he introduced me to his foreman. I was hired on the spot. Mack did have to tell him I was a nephew, because I was under eighteen. There seemed to be some kind of union rule about hiring relatives, as opposed to off the street.

I contacted City College, the place from which my correspondence courses came, and made arrangements to take eight more courses. If there was a charge for them, I was never told. They must have charged the school I had just left. My first high school principal had laid out an agenda. The correspondence school had a copy of it, and they gave me the course subjects he had suggested. There were times when I had a choice, between two or three subjects, but the agenda was always followed. I thought I didn't have a choice. The courses came to Mack's address two weeks later, with instructions to contact the local high school so they could administer the final tests.

I slept under a tree in Mack's yard and took my meals with him. During the day we helped repair, and maintain, a section of track about forty miles long. In the evenings I was studying, fishing, or hunting. We went to work very early, so our eight hours were over early in the afternoon, and we were off on weekends. I seemed to have a lot of spare time.

Mack had an old bicycle that he let me ride. One day I was riding down a game trail in the woods. The brush was thick, so I could not see around some of the corners. When I rounded one of those corners, I found myself face to face with a moose. I stopped the bicycle and stood there. We had a staring contest for about two minutes. It seemed much longer. The moose, finally, moved away. I started to peddle the bike back to the house, but discovered that, when I stopped so suddenly, I had broken the chain.

That year I bought my first automobile. It was a 1936 Chevrolet. All Mack had was a flat bed truck, so we began using my car to go to work, and to town. In order to get away for peace and quiet I had a habit of driving way up into the mountains on weekends. I spent hours there, studying, beside a mountain stream.

It was on one of those excursions that I met a man everyone said was crazy, but I found interesting.

60

He was an old prospector that had found a pocket of copper ore. When the mine played out, he stayed. He once told me that the reason everyone thought he was crazy was because they believed he was still digging for the big strike. In actual fact, he was there because he owned the place and he liked it. He had not been in the old mine in years.

I stayed overnight with him several times. The first time we had oatmeal for breakfast. He put something in the mush that looked like ground raisins, but was sweet. When I asked what it was, he told me "It's ants. If you want sweet you eat ants". He would take a plastic bag, and a stick, to an anthill. The ant was a large reddish brown variety that was plentiful in the area. He would get some ants on the stick and shake them off into the bag. Then he would crush the ants with a rolling pin. When he had all of the ants he needed, he would lay them out to dry and then store them in a small jar.

He taught me other things as well. We made furniture out of logs and rawhide. We even made a door the same way. We wove baskets and mats from cattails. We tanned hides and made things from the leather. My studies suffered, but I was getting another type of education. That old mountain man taught me a lot of what I know of wilderness survival. I honed those skills over the years, but he was my teacher. I never knew his name, nor did anyone I ever met. He was just "that crazy old prospector". He certainly never mentioned it and I was too polite to ask.

School was one weekend away when the section hand job ended. I reported to the school and made arrangements to be tested. The Principal was uncooperative, but I found one teacher who was enthusiastic about it. She became my mentor and acted on my behalf with the principal. He seemed to have taken one look at me and decided I wasn't worth his time.

That year I started to take a class in journalism. Almost every English class I ever attended wanted everyone to write a story about their summer as soon as school started. I wrote a wild yarn about fighting Indians and being a cowboy. The teacher liked it, and so did the class. I was asked to write a series of yarns for the school paper. The principal was the journalism teacher. He kicked me out of class because he didn't like the way I abbreviated United States of America. I had less than a week of journalism, yet years later I owned, and published a newspaper. Life takes some strange twists at times. He, also flunked me in history. At the time I had accumulated several college credits in the subject. In later years I earned a degree in history. I retook American History the next year and never opened the book. I got an "A".

That winter I became a "professional hunter". My twenty-two supplied meat for Mack and three neighbors. The next-door neighbor was Mack's sister and her family. They had a son a year or so older than me, but he was a lazy bum. Mack said he couldn't hit the side of a barn with a baseball bat if he was standing next to it. There were five in that family.

Next to them was Mack's niece and her children. Her husband was in the Army. Further down the road one more house was where the widows lived. There were two of them, sisters, living together. All in all I provided meat for eleven people on a regular basis, and a couple more families on occasion.

My current mentor, Mrs. Chase, was only able to convince the principal to let me take two correspondence courses per semester. Therefore I had more than the normal amount of free time. Since I had a car, I became prone to go into town. The boy next door introduced me to some of his friends. Like him, most of them were "drop-outs". They all worked in the summer, but once the snows came the sawmills closed down and work became scarce. They had plenty of time to think up mischief.

During one of their parties, out by a frozen lake, I got into a fight with one of those drunks. His knife got me across the wrist. I fell to the ground on my back and kicked out. My foot caught him in the crotch. By the time the pain had subsided enough for him to stand straight and talk, he was sober. The fight was over. We walked back to the campfire together.

A big guy I had never seen at any of their "shindigs" came over and wrapped my handkerchief around my wound. He said his name was, Kevin. We talked for a couple hours. Neither one of us were particularly interested in the party, so we decided to go back to town. I had ridden out there with someone else because Mack was using my car. His truck was not running. Kevin had to have been at least six feet, four inches tall. He was about my age and, like most of the others, had quit school.

We got about half way to town when an axle broke on his car. We had to walk the ten, or more, miles back to his parents' house. We arrived about five o'clock in the morning and he insisted that I stay there. I hit the sack in a big, soft, feather bed. It was the first time I had been so comfortable in my life. I didn't want to leave all that comfort, but I got up about ten. Kevin was just coming out of his room, so we went down stairs together.

Kevin's mother was waiting with a big breakfast. The rest of the family had eaten, and left for work, several hours earlier. His mother was only about five feet tall, and very round. She reminded me of Mother Wright. When she saw the wound on my wrist, and the dirty handkerchief we used for a bandage, she "hit the roof". She said we should have done something about it a lot earlier. She washed it, and bandaged my wrist with clean gauze, fussing over me like I was her own. Late that afternoon she introduced me to Kevin's father. He was half a head taller than Kevin. I learned that there were six sons in the family. In the words of Kevin's dad, "each one is bigger than the other". Kevin, at six, four and two hundred and forty pounds, was the runt of the "litter" according to his mother.

Kevin's dad showed me something that I can still see over forty years later. It was a ruby arrowhead. It was a small one, called a bird point, and red as blood. A chain of gold nuggets, each about the size of a pea, was attached to it. Between each nugget was one small link. The chain was eighteen inches long. Two of his sons had found the arrowhead in the woods, not far from there. His two oldest sons owned a gold claim in Alaska. Every summer they went up there to work the claim. They stole the arrowhead and took it with them. When they came back, in the fall, they stopped in Seattle and had the chain made. (Almost thirty years later I was buying an engagement ring from the Jeweler friend of my fiancé's family. I told him about the arrowhead, and the chain. He said he was the man that made that chain and that the arrowhead was priceless. As a ruby it was worth about five thousand dollars, at the time he made the chain, but, as an arrowhead, there was no way to put a price on it.)

Kevin's family was an interesting enigma. I learned, once again, that the way people perceive others, and their reputation is often somewhat different from the truth. By reputation they were an uneducated, ignorant, bunch of backward hillbillies. It was said that they had cut a hole in the floor of one of their closets, and used it as an indoor toilet. They were supposed to be anything but honest, and were to be avoided at all cost. Even in that rough lumbering society they were outcasts.

The truth was entirely different. It was true that they took a couple closets and converted them to bathrooms. When the house was built there were no bathroom facilities put in houses. It was true that the outside of the house was rough. There were a lot of cars parked around the yard, and there were several trash barrels around. With that many drivers, and that many big eaters, it was no wonder there were a lot of those things. Inside, the home was immaculately clean, with nothing but the best in furniture. Even then, feather beds were expensive. Every one in the family had one, and one in the spare bedroom. The place was so big that each boy had his own bedroom. I counted ten bedrooms in the place, plus a massive living room and a kitchen that easily accommodated the entire family. Their kitchen table was at least ten feet long and five feet wide, and solid oak. They may not have had a lot of formal education, but they were far from being ignorant, and they were rich. They had more money than they could ever spend, and they were far richer in another way, they had love.

The men of the family all drank liquor, but were not drunkards. When they went to the bar, there were some who would want to fight them because of their mild manners. They always won their fights, once they were pushed into one. If any of those boys had picked a fight, even though they were full grown, their dad would have "fixed their wagon" when they got home.

They were a wonderful family, with a lot of love between them. I have always wished that I could have seen more of my new friend, but circumstances, in both of our lives, prevented it.

Late in February, I was driving around late at night with sixteen teenagers in my car. That is a lot, in a two-door sedan. We were stuck in snow banks eighteen times. I got frostbite on both feet, my hands, and my nose. I decided it was time to settle down, and concentrate on my studies once again. I finished my extra courses and left that town in March, to get to a warmer climate.

10.

I stopped in a small town in Utah, because I had a flat tire. The man at the service station offered me a job, so I stayed. I had missed nearly a week of school when I enrolled at the local high school. The principal was more than helpful when I asked for the next correspondence courses on my agenda. Three weeks later he called me into his office. He asked how I was progressing with the three subjects I had selected. I told him I was nearly half done with them. Then he informed me that I had all the credits I needed to graduate, except two: American History, and another physical education class. He said the history could be waived because I had already passed college courses in the subject with very good grades. He advised me that, in the last year of high school I should take physical education only, and concentrate on the correspondence school's courses.

When I mentioned that I might not be in his school, or even the same state, when school started again. He told me he would take care of it for me. He got me a copy of my transcript and wrote a letter. I was instructed to give it to the principal of my next school. The envelope was sealed so I could not read what he had written and he made me promise not to try getting into it.

School let out at the end of May. I left town on the first of June. The people there were good to me, and I had a good job, but everyone was trying to get me to join their church. I had nothing against their religion, at the time, but I didn't want to be a Mormon. They had too many restrictions.

I drove north again, hoping to go back to work on the railroad. I landed a job on the "extra gang" and became a "gandy dancer". Like before, the job was repairing tracks. The extra gang made major repairs, replacing miles of old railroad ties and laying new rails. It was hard, backbreaking work, but the pay was good. They made us live in boxcars right on the job site and didn't allow the men to have cars. I sold my old Chevrolet to an acquaintance who paid half and promised to send me the rest. I never got it.

Every weekend we got paid and all of the men would go to town and get drunk. Some of them didn't make it back, so there was a constant flow of new men to take their places. I was too young, and not prone to drunken binges, so I stayed back, with my "nose in a book". At first, they called me "kid". Then it was "book worm". This changed to "perfesser" and to a couple of names I don't care to remember. The job ended late in July.

I wandered south again. I attended a rodeo in Kansas and ran into my rodeo stock rancher friend. He suggested that I try rodeoing, so I joined the rodeo "circuit". He said he would teach me to "rodeo", but my job was to drive one of the trucks between shows, and help with the stock. I rode saddle broncs and bareback. The first few times I ate a lot of dirt. I, quickly, learned how to fall off without getting something broken. After a lot of tutoring I began to stay on the back of the horse long enough to "get time". I had a lot of fun, but I never made much money. I won "day money" once in a while and even took first place a time or two. I still have a belt buckle I won at one of those rodeos.

The circuit went north and ended up on Labor Day in Miles City, Montana. We got there a day early so, my boss and I took a drive toward the east of the city. We were just driving around as relaxation. We got to a small town with a high school right beside the highway. I said I liked the looks of the building so we went in and talked to the principal. I rented a small house out in an open field not far from school. The boss paid me the wages I had earned, wished me luck and said he would have my belongings brought out after the rodeo was over. When I got home from school after the first day, my things were on the front porch.

Because of my transcript, I was only required to take physical education, but I elected to take American History as well. I was still festering about that failure. When the Principal learned what I had been doing for a living, he commented that he would like to give me credit for having all the physical education I needed, but state requirements would not allow it. He handed me a permanent excuse from classes, at my own discretion. His only requirement was that I take, and pass, all tests.

I loaded up with correspondence courses. My new Principal was behind me all the way. I could not have asked for a better Mentor. I took as many as eight courses at a time. It seemed like a heavy load, on the surface, but I got along fine. A five credit hour course, in college, means that there are five hours of class each week for one semester, plus homework. Most colleges will tell you that there is a minimum of one hour homework for each credit hour. The needed material is in the text, or the libraries, in most colleges; not in the class. My courses were from three to five credit hour courses. I spent from ten to twelve hours a day, seven days a week, studying. I did it because I enjoyed it. I never really cared what I was studying, although some courses were more enjoyable than others. I was following the curriculum laid out by my first high school principal. When that was completed, I started taking courses that I thought would be interesting. I had no car, no friends, no interest in sports, and was shy around girls.

In all the years I went to High School I had only one date. One night I double dated with a guy and his girl. Her parents wouldn't let her go out unless there was another couple along. They fixed me up with a cute blonde girl I thought I liked. We went to a movie. During the show she took my hand and guided it to her lap, under her coat. She started rubbing herself between her legs with my hand. Then she whispered in my ear, "I like that". I was so shocked, and shy, that I didn't know what to do.

On the way back to her house we sat in the back of the car. She sat on my lap with her coat over our laps. Her dress was up around her waist and I had my hand just where she wanted it placed. I saw her again a few days later, only this time we were alone. She initiated the same kind of play. This time things progressed to their logical conclusion. It was over almost before it began. I was a little disappointed and wondered what the big deal was, about sex. By the time I went to school on Monday, everyone knew what we had done. She had complained to one of her girlfriends about being sore, and said why. She didn't want anything to do with me after that one night. I went back to being a recluse. The experience didn't turn me off on girls, but it sure turned me off on that one and delayed my entrance into "the joys of male/female relationships".

The high school had a "College Day" for the seniors. I decided to go, even though I could never afford college. I met Howard Porter, the owner of Billings Business College, in Billings Montana. He was very impressed with my academics and promised to give me a job in his school, as janitor, if I would attend his classes. He said, "You'll be surprised at what I can do for you". I decided I liked that man, and promised I would be there when his classes started in the spring. I enrolled for classes, starting the day after graduation, but something interfered.

I don't know what triggered it, but in March of that year I got to thinking that I wanted to go home. I wanted the Wrights to see me graduate from high school. As time went on the feeling got stronger. I finished up the courses I was taking and took off for Texas. I arrived early in May. I registered at the high school in Farmer's Branch and went out to surprise the folks.

Big George, and Mother Wright were so sick that they didn't recognize me at first. When they did, they hardly had the strength to welcome me back. I could tell they were glad to see me, but their weak smiles were filled with pain. A neighbor, I didn't know, was looking after them and she greeted me as a welcome relief to some of her burden. This I did gladly. I went to school to finish the history and physical education requirements and returned each day before noon. The Principal assured me that he would send for my school records and I would be able to graduate. I hoped the Wrights could see it. I wanted them to be proud of me.

The cancer took Mother Wright first. Big George never shed a tear. He just gave up. He was dead in three days. Mother Wright's last few words to me were to keep the family Bible. She said it contained a record of family history and she didn't want a stranger to have it. I have always believed that it was my only opportunity to discover my real identity, but it was not to be.

Big George died just after I left for school. By the time I got home, at eleven, an officer of the law was there. The doctors that had been tending the Wrights seized everything, including my personal belongings. In a gesture of good will he let me take a couple of changes of clothes, but it was against his orders. When I tried to take the Bible he stopped me. He handed me a bill for over forty thousand dollars.

I went to the attorney that had taken out the papers, in behalf of the doctors. I was informed, in no uncertain terms, that the house, land, and everything on the premises now belonged to the doctors. He would not even consider letting me have that Bible. He threatened to take me to court if I didn't pay the bill they had given me, as next of kin. I got mad. There was a shouting match, and a threat of physical violence. I told that lawyer just exactly where he could put his invoice and his lawsuit. I was taken out of the office by a policeman.

The policeman calmed me down and talked to be about the situation. Once outside, he told me that it was none of his business, and he would get into trouble if I said anything. He said he was a forth year law student and he could tell me that the bill was probably uncollectible since it was quite obvious that I was not a relative. He said I would save myself a lot of grief, and a lot of money, if I left town. There was no lawsuit filed at the moment, and I was free to leave. He said the worst thing that could happen was that the property would be taken, by court order, and that would happen anyway. The only thing I could possibly gain would be my own personal possessions. He thought the whole thing was a smokescreen, to prevent any complications in their takeover of the property. I took his advice, but I hated to leave my twenty-two, the old army blanket, and the family Bible.

I went out to the farm that night. I was going to enter the house and retrieve my belongings and the Bible. They were expecting me to do just that. The house was completely vacant. During the day they had taken the furniture and everything. The house had a lock on the doors, with a legal notice tacked up. I was able to go through the very window I escaped from when I was a kid, and retrieve some money I had stashed in a secret place under a floorboard that was loose. I slept on the floor. My final tests at school were done, and the grades were in, yet it was a few days before the graduation ceremony. I decided to go ahead and go to Business College. I, actually, had no choice. I had to get out of town before I was arrested for trespassing. I did not sleep well, so I was out of the house by five in the morning. I was not a hundred yards from the farm when a security vehicle entered the yard and two security guards started looking around the place. I left for Billings Montana exactly one week before graduation. I gave the school's address to the Principal, who assured me that he would mail my diploma. I never got it.

11.

Once in Billings, I started a concentrated nine month course in accounting. True to his word, Mr. Porter hired me as school janitor. This paid my tuition and books. He helped me find a job, working in the offices of a large wholesale hardware corporation after school and found me an apartment. I never knew, for sure, but I think he did more than that. All of my records were assembled, from all of the various correspondence courses. Most of them were from City College. Once all of the records were submitted, and verified, City College mailed a Bachelors of Business Administration Diploma to my address. I got my degree within days of my graduation from the business college.

The degree came as a surprise to me. I had never had it in my mind, but that first high school principal evidently did. Mr. Porter took me into his office and pointed out a few credits I had that could be used toward my advanced degree. He said I was not that far away from it and urged me to go for my Masters. He paid for four more advanced courses as a means of encouragement.

It was difficult for an eighteen-year-old, even one with a degree, to find work. One day I happened to meet an independent truck driver. He hired me to set up an accounting system for him. A few days later we went on the road to see if my system was adequate. Officially I was his "relief driver". I actually drove a lot less than his logbook showed. I got that job by accident.

He asked me if I could drive. I said yes, so he told me to back his tractor trailer rig into a loading dock between two other rigs. I had watched him going through the gears earlier in the day, when we were discussing his bookkeeping system. I cranked the rig around and lined it up. Then I backed toward the dock. When I thought I was close enough, by looking at the other trucks, I hit the air brakes. I was less than two inches from the dock. He thought I could do the job. I never did tell him that I had never driven an eighteen wheeler before that day. We were on the road a little over six weeks before we got back to Billings.

I checked in with Mr. Porter and took a couple of tests. Then I started looking for a job again. I was walking by the Army Recruiting office one day and decided to talk to them. Before I left the office, I had enlisted. I had one week to wind up any business matters that were necessary. I took the time to finish my remaining correspondence courses.

Two days after I enlisted, Mr. Porter called me. He had a position for me, as payroll accountant for a large construction company. We were both disappointed that I had joined the Army. Once in the military I was able to have the government pay for my education. The various High Schools paid for most of my correspondence courses through that period. The only ones that cost me money were the ones the school could not, or would not authorize.

According to the papers I signed when I joined, I was supposed to be in the Criminal Investigation Department of the Army, after basic training. During basic I took the tests, and went before the board, to go to Officer's Candidate School. Much to my surprise, I got it. I tried hard, to be the best soldier in the outfit. I never went on a pass, except one time. About six of us went to Juarez Mexico from Fort Bliss, Texas, during basic training. I remember that a friend and I went to a bar and sat on the barstools while he had a drink of beer, and I had some soda. He got a "dose of crabs", but I didn't.

Luck, and being in the right place, has a lot to do with things at times. During Officer's Candidate School we were on a field exercise firing 90MM guns. Near each gun emplacement was a deep hole. In case of a misfire, the live cannon shell was to be dumped in the pit, just in case it exploded. I found out that their caution was justified. I was standing with a group of other candidates, watching a firing demonstration, when the gun in the next emplacement misfired. Everyone was running for cover and yelling. In my excitement, fear, or confusion, I ran over and opened the breach. As the shell fell out I cradled it in my arms and ran. Throwing the shell into the pit, I hit the ground. It dropped into the pit just as it exploded. No one was hurt. The training officer come over and put his hand on my shoulder. He said, "good job son. It could have killed all of us". That was all I ever heard about the incident.

Officer's Candidate School had another month, before graduation, when it was announced that one candidate would be able to graduate with the rank of First Lieutenant, instead of Second Lieutenant. The man was to be chosen, by the Base Commander, for his scholarship, ability as an officer, and his self-discipline under stress. I never thought of myself as being any better, as a candidate, than any man in the class. I have always felt that in spite of how hard I tried to be the best that I could be, I got that promotion because of the incident on the firing range, and not because I deserved it.

After O.C.S., all newly commissioned officers were required to take either paratrooper training, or ranger training. I didn't like the idea of jumping out of airplanes so I signed up for the rangers. They made me jump anyway, as part of ranger training. During that training we were sent on a survival mission. We were dropped into a wilderness area and told to make our way out to a base camp. Some of my early training came in handy. We were a team of two men. We arrived at the base camp first, and in good shape. My partner even gained some weight. Most of the others were nearly starved and did not look as though they had been on a Sunday picnic.

After ranger training, the Army was true to it's word. I went into classes for the Criminal Investigation Department. We learned how to conduct an investigation, collect evidence, and preserve a crime scene. It was all to no avail. Somewhere along the line someone read my records. I went from school to my first assignment; auditing books, and records. After the "bull in a china closet" methods of the Military Police failed, I was the guy they sent in, to find out what was happening. Instead of threat and intimidation, we used undercover investigation. In most instances there was, actually, no crime. Usually, it was "human error".

At an Army payroll center we discovered that there were people working there that couldn't add very well. The money that was supposed to be missing, uncovered by a previous audit, wasn't. Another time there was no theft of weapons, as reported. A clerk typist had listed several serial numbers more than once. It took a whole day to find that one, and another day to convince the Military Police that they were wrong.

All officers, in the military, must have a "secret" clearance. Since most of my work was with classified material, my commanding officer requested that my clearance be upgraded to the highest classification. When my "Q" clearance was approved most of my work was classified. It was at that time that I gave up any hope of ever finding my true family. The thorough background check the FBI conducts, when giving such a clearance would have turned up something, if the information was available.

My work was interesting, easy, and sporadic. A job might last a day, a week, or a month, but in between assignments I sat around for a few days, or a few weeks. It was perfect for my avocation, studying. Eventually I was notified that I had completed all of the requirement for my Masters of Business Administration degree, except one. I needed to write my graduating thesis. The school helped me with that problem.

I was contacted by a man who was working on his doctorate. I could help him, while completing my own work. He had the contacts, subject, and an outline. I took the thirty days leave I had coming, and borrowed another thirty. When my commanding officer was informed of what I planned, he was more than willing to help by approving the leave.

The subject of the thesis was the affect of music, in the workplace. My area had to do with time and efficiency, in a labor-intensive environment where the two are important. I worked with a cartage company at night. One of the men was also a student in the daytime. I gave him a dollar an hour to help me. It was not a bad deal. He made a dollar an hour more than anyone else who worked at night, except the foreman. Because of union rules, I was also paid, but I never requested it. The company was very cooperative, and created an opening for me, so I could do the thesis.

Every night the boxes for delivery the next day were unloaded from the trucks that brought them in. They were marked with a number and sent down a conveyer belt. At several different locations a man would pick the numbers, for which he was responsible, off the belt and set them on the floor. Another man had the manifest for the trucks they were to load. As the boxes were set aside, he put them in order according to his manifest. When this was done the trucks were loaded in the order of delivery, so that the first ones to be delivered would be near the rear door.

We played a different kind of music in each of four locations. The fifth had no music at all. We kept accurate records, and switched the music each group heard from one day to the next so that each group experienced all four sounds, and none. Once the routine was repeated several times we collated our information and drew our conclusions. None of the other employees were told what we were doing, or even that we were doing anything.

The most effective sound, for both speed and accuracy, was Classical music; followed by "Elevator", none, Country, and Rock and Roll, in that order. It took me a week to type up the resulting thesis. I mailed it in the day I reported back to my Commanding Officer, for duty. Orders were waiting for me. I was off to Korea for a tour that lasted almost a year and would change my life around one more time.

12.

I was in Korea a month before my "Sheepskin" arrived. I now had my Masters Degree in Business Administration. My studies didn't stop there. I had always liked history, and had a number of credits toward that degree, so I started more extensive studies in that area. The Army was footing the bill, so I loaded up with courses. My work in Korea was not overly demanding so I had a lot of free time. I managed to take up photography, and even took a course in mechanical drawing. Then came an interesting assignment.

There are times when events just seem to happen. We do our jobs as best we can and circumstances seem to happen without any control. I guess you could call it fate or coincidence but I think of it more as the luck of the draw. This time we drew two cards to a royal flush.

The Korean C.I.D. had notified us that there seemed to be a larger than normal amount of American goods on the black market. Service men had a habit of buying things at the post exchange and selling them on the street, especially cigarettes. Although not legal the offence had always been overlooked unless blatant. What was happening now was a flooding of the market, of PX merchandise. Truckloads of American Army stores had to have been sold.

I was the Officer in Charge of a two man team. The team was ordered to conduct audits of the several warehouses in the Pusan area in an effort to discover whether the goods were coming from the U.S. Army.

The team consisted of M/Sgt. Corbin, a career man with eighteen years in the army. To look at him one would picture a bricklayer, or a construction laborer but when he spoke you might think more of a college professor. He had taken courses in accounting through correspondence and knew exactly what to look for. Corbin was just Corbin to everyone who knew him. Few people had ever heard his first name.

We were teamed together when we first arrived in Korea. Actually we had both been on the same ship from the States. We became friends during the trip because of a mutual interest in chess. I had the ration breakdown detail for the troop ship and Corbin was my Sergeant. Our job was to requisition the day's food, for meals, from the hold. Eight enlisted men would pull the supplies and deliver them to the mess—or galley. Corbin and I spent the day eating fig Newton's, and ice cream, and playing chess.

After our arrival in Korea we walked into headquarters together, and were given the assignment as a team of experts. We thought of it as a "gravy job". We could avoid any of the hard criminal activity and take it easy.

The investigation into the black marketing netted nothing for almost three months. Then 83 days into the project, we started on the second to the last warehouse. The second day into the audit I noticed there were more than what would be considered normal shipments to one post exchange, and all signed by a M/Sgt Davids. We decided to check the location personally just to see if the shipments were authorized. Two hours later and almost thirty miles north of Pusan we arrived at our destination. We expected to find a large base with an equally large exchange. We were in for a little surprise.

It was an old army ordinance depot that had been vacated for a long time. The few buildings that were left were deserted, except for the rats. Weeds grew everywhere, and there was a sign posted by the government of Korea that read, "No Trespassing" in Korean, and English. The lock on the gate was broken and we could see the tracks of vehicles leading to the only usable building in the compound. The building was vacant, but locked with an almost new lock. When we returned to the office we had our usual progress reports typed and sent to headquarters. For the next three days we continued with our investigation, gathering more information as to specifically what was shipped and how much of each item.

We also started a check of the service records of all the men working at the warehouse. At 0800 hours on the fourth day I received a telephone call from headquarters telling me to pick up the M/Sgt. Written orders would follow. It looked like we nailed one by auditing the books. At 0810 hours we received the requested service records. Something did not ring true.

That Master Sergeant was a veteran of 16 years with an outstanding record. He was wounded in the last days of WWII and again in the Korean conflict. Both Corbin and I felt he should be given the benefit of the doubt and further investigation was required. We felt, with his record, he could not have been so dishonest. Two Purple Hearts, a Silver Star, several letters of commendation and 16 years just didn't add up to a crook. I told headquarters we still had some evidence to collect and it would take another three or four days. In order to have a Court Martial, in the Army, the evidence must be very good, so headquarters agreed.

We continued to investigate. We hung around the warehouse looking at first one record and then another, gathering volumes of material, and getting the routine of the place. In the next three days we had a complete record including dates, amounts and items that were stolen. All that remained was a check of the dates the various personnel were assigned to the warehouse. Anyone assigned there after the thefts started would be a poor suspect. It came as no surprise to discover there were no shipments to the old ordinance depot and everyone was the picture of efficiency from the beginning of the audit. Twenty-seven men worked there counting the Officer in Charge, a Lieutenant. A Master Sergeant, a Corporal and twenty-four Privates completed the roster. The Lieutenant and the Master Sergeant were the only ones authorized to sign outgoing invoices and approve requisitions.

The Lieutenant was a college man who got his commission through the ROTC. program. He was not married and was somewhat of a playboy. We discovered that he had seldom been at his post and was spending a lot of time with his Korean girlfriend. Other than that, the Lieutenant seemed clean but derelict in his duties. It began to look more and more as though the M/Sgt was our man. Pressure was building up to do something. Headquarters began to think we were dragging our feet. The investigation had taken 105 days and that was too long.

Word was passed down from my good friend, the clerk typist at the Far East Command Headquarters in Japan. "The General got hold of this and wants action". I had a Major for a boss. The Major's boss was a "Bird" Colonel and his boss was the General.

The General was in charge of all C.I.D. operations in the Far East and had a reputation for being a thorough investigator that demanded complete documentation and conclusive evidence before any action could be taken. My clerk typist friend informed me that I had until Monday or Tuesday since he had learned directly from the General's office and written orders were coming through channels.

It was a cold Friday night in November. Not being much of a sleeper anyway, and bothered about the investigation, I decided to go for a long walk just to think about things. You could not call it "taking the night air" since at that time Pusan was the largest city in the world without a sewer system. This activity was nothing unusual as I often went for walks late at night after the city calmed down, and the streets were more or less deserted. My travels took me from Pier 1 up through Pusan proper until I found myself, at 0230, in an area off limits to military personnel. This didn't worry me as I had been there several times before. The main street wasn't dangerous but the side streets definitely were. Many soldiers had lost their money, and sometimes their lives in the area. I was armed and, because of my position in the C.I.D., authorized to be there.

Just as I started to pass a narrow street known, for obviously good reasons by every American Soldier, as Gonorrhea Alley I heard scuffling and an American voice calling for help. I thought, "Oh Great, another soldier wandered off where he shouldn't be and is getting rolled! Will those guys ever learn there is a reason this place is off limits". The street was about twenty feet wide, and lighted only by the lights from the windows of several whorehouses, and bars, along the way. Not knowing what I was getting into I drew my weapon and stepped into the street. Someone had to pull that idiot's fat out of the fire!

I stepped around a pile of baskets, with gun in hand, to see, about 25 feet away, a soldier on the ground with two big Koreans over him. There was the flash of steel. They had some very wicked looking knives and were about to strike. That poor fool was as good as dead!

The first shot from my 38 special took one Korean just behind the left ear. He dropped like a falling tree right on top of the hapless man on the ground. The noise, and the sudden fall of the first man, took the second by surprise. He looked up just in time to take the second round between the eyes, about an inch up from the eyebrows. The impact threw him against the wall of a building. He slid down the wall, and his dead body sat there like a passed out drunk.

Seconds later I was rolling the dead Korean off the poor slob on the ground. "You alright?" I said, as I helped the man up, and gathered my thoughts. I was going to give him a royal "ass chewing" for being there in the first place. Then I was going to call the Military Police. As I helped him up the reflection of the lighted windows showed a single star on the shoulder of the "fool".

All thought of chewing out this man vanished with amazement. "What is a General doing here this time of night?" All I could manage to choke out was, "get your ass out of here fast!" Without a word, the General left in a hurry. What he was doing there, or who he was, or where he went, I never even wanted to know. The report went in as an unidentified American serviceman. The General could not have known who saved him that night. C.I.D. personnel wore only an olive green uniform with no insignia other than the U.S. on each lapel, no designation of rank and no nametag.

So much for Friday night—or better yet, Saturday morning very early. By the time I finished typing the shooting report it was just after o-four hundred hours. I slept soundly for three hours before Corbin was pounding on my door. Over breakfast, we talked about the shooting, but I never mentioned the General. We went back to the office to discuss the investigation.

Reluctantly we decided there was no choice other than to charge the M/Sgt. with theft of government property. The Clerk Typist started on the papers. It would take him a long time because of the regulations. There can be no errors, strikeovers, or erasures on Court Martial papers. Even though it was Saturday afternoon we decided to get things started and have it done by Monday morning. It's not a good idea to make all your bosses mad—all the way up to the Far East Commander. Orders were coming, within the next two days, and we wanted the jump on them.

It was Sunday, and the paperwork was almost done when a telephone call came in. There was a fire at the warehouse! The O.I.C. (Officer in Charge) at the fire department thought it prudent to call when he noticed a strong gasoline smell, even though there was no gasoline stored near the warehouse. On the way over we decided it would be a good idea to pick up the Lieutenant. He was not in, probably with his girl or at the Officers Club. We went to the Master Sergeants barracks, but were informed that he was in town somewhere, so we proceeded toward the warehouse. About four blocks from the warehouse we noticed the Corporal that worked under the Master Sergeant. He did not seem too happy to see two C.I.D. investigators when the jeep stopped—probably because he reeked of gasoline.

Corbin had a habit of always carrying a small tape recorder. He turned it on as I ordered the Corporal into the jeep. It only took one breath to smell the fuel. I asked, "Well Corporal why did you start a fire at the warehouse?" He said, "What fire?" Corbin said, "The one you started! You are four blocks away, and going away from the biggest fire you've ever seen. You smell of gas and smoke. Answer the Lieutenant!" When a Master Sergeant that looks like he could eat you for breakfast asks a question in the tone of voice Corbin used there usually are results.

At this point there was no proof of arson or of the Corporal's involvement in arson, but assumption sometimes pays off. He confessed. He said, "Alright I did it". By this time we had arrived at the fire. Corbin asked the big question. Why? The answer startled both of us. "Because you were getting too close."

A glance showed that the recorder was still recording. We showed no emotion. "As a matter of fact we were just preparing the papers for a Court Martial" said Corbin, not bothering to say whom the papers would charge. I said, "Why don't you just tell us all about it, beginning with why you started stealing and ending with this fire."

The Cpl. joined the Army to keep from going to jail. A judge in the Midwest ordered him to enlist in hopes that the Army could do what parents and civilian government could not. He had an arrest record going back to when he was 10 years old, mostly petty theft. In the Army he was suspected in three different cases but never charged. He had been in the service for 17 months when assigned to the warehouse detail. Promoted to Corporal because of time in grade, and to fill a vacancy, he found himself in a good position. All he had to do was to learn the routine, study the Master Sergeant's signature and set up his distribution system.

He started with just a few items, which he carried out himself, until he contacted a Korean with access to an Army vehicle from during the conflict. The Korean informed him that he and his associates would take all they could get. The Korean was the one who came up with the old ordinance depot. When his big break in the black market came, the Cpl. was using the Master Sergeant's name and was wearing the proper clothing. The gang of Korean criminals thought they were doing business with the wrong man.

Business started booming! He typed phony requisitions, shipped merchandise to his phony ordinance depot and signed The Master Sergeant's name to every one of them. He told us he knew it could have been proved that the Sergeant had not signed some of the shipping orders and that would prove he was guilty. Shipments were made when the Master Sergeant was in Japan on R & R (Rest and Recuperation). When we pulled those particular records he thought his luck had run out. We had not discovered this piece of evidence. To cover his tracks he went to the warehouse, dumped all the records in the middle of the floor and doused them with gasoline. He then fashioned a wick out of gas and a rope, started it on fire and left the building.

If he had not stayed for a while, to watch from across the street, and ran into us, he probably would have gotten away a while longer. He knew the M/Sgt was not in the barracks and would probably not be able to account for his whereabouts. He had slipped the Sergeant a "Mickey", and he was sleeping it off in the bedroom of a whore. He had succeeded in destroying everything. All records, the warehouse and it's contents, over half of a million dollars was destroyed by the arson.

Once we deposited the prisoner with the Military Police, we went back to the office and rewrote the report and Court Martial Papers. The Clerk Typist had finished his job and had gone when we arrived. We waited until Monday morning to give him the news that he would have to start all over again. Monday morning I called my boss, the major, and gave an oral report. The typewritten report was sent through channels to the Far East Commander. We took the rest of the day to celebrate.

One week later I was a Captain. Master Sergeant Corbin went from E-7 to E-8. The incident in the alley was never investigated, and all records disappeared. The warehouse case was blown all out of proportion, which resulted in promotions long before they were due. Two C.I.D. investigators decided not to argue with the results.

The Corporal got forty years for Arson, theft of government property, forgery, profiteering on the black market and various other charges. The M/Sgt got a reprimand, and a transfer for not keeping an eye on things. The Lieutenant was reprimanded but kept his job and lost his girlfriend. The Koreans involved were all rounded up by the Korean C.I.D.. No one knows what happened but most of them, and a couple government officials, were found dead by various means and under mysterious circumstances.

Five years after leaving the service I got "the rest of the story". An old friend, Mr. Lee, happened to be in Seattle at a Police Chief's convention. We met, by chance, in one of the better "watering holes" one evening and I told him my side of the Gonorrhea Alley incident. He gave me the missing pieces. The General in charge of the Far East C.I.D. had contacted him and told his story. Lee gave my name as the only one who would have been in the area at the time of the incident. When I made out the shooting incident report the General knew.

The General had decided to do some investigation on his own. He decided to approach the depot theft case from the other end so the entire operation could be stopped. He arranged a meeting with the head of the Korean C.I.D., the Chief of Police and the Mayor of Pusan. They agreed to meet him at a secret place in downtown Pusan.

At the meeting the Korean C.I.D. man introduced him to Mr. Lee, the Chief of Police, and Mr. Kim Ling, the Mayor of Pusan. Two informants were brought in. They told the General that the contact in the military was the Master Sergeant. They gave details that were confirmed by Lee and Ling as being fact. The meeting started at 2300 hours and was not ended until nearly 0230 the following morning. The General had all the proof he needed as he left the meeting on that cold November morning in downtown Pusan. First thing Monday morning he would throw a M/Sgt. in the guardhouse, and read the riot act to a couple C.I.D. investigators.

He was just leaving his meeting place when he was approached by the two informants he had met earlier. Thinking they had something else to tell him he greeted them warmly—then they attacked. He fought them off until he stumbled on a protruding piece of cobblestone and went down. Involuntarily, he called for help! Someone started shooting. One of the Koreans fell on top of him and the other was thrown against the building. A couple seconds later he was being helped up. His rescuer asked, "You okay", but before he could answer he heard a gasp and then, "get your ass out of here."

13.

Once the "dust settled" from that case we had some time off. I "hit the books" while my partner took some well-deserved R and R in Japan. It was a good thing I worked so hard to finish those history courses. I was given a job to do that was classified so highly that not even my boss, or even his boss, knew about it. Orders were sent, relieving me of all duties and to have me available for T.D.Y. (Temporary Duty) assignments as ordered by the Department of the Army.

My boss's boss was a full Bird Colonel and knew better than to question orders. From that point until the day I was returned to the United States, and certain other periods of time my life there is a complete void. It's not that I can't remember or that I don't know. When I am about seventy I might be able to talk about that time without fear of reprisal. Fifty years after the fact might be how long it takes some things to get declassified, but it never gets forgotten. I'll tell that story in another book.

There is a reason the government of the United States has one political party with a jackass for a symbol, another with an elephant, and a national bird of prey, the eagle, for a symbol. The government is stubborn as a jackass, never forgets, watches everything from high up, and swoops down to attack with vicious claws. I am patriotic or I never would have consented to do the things I did, but I am also a realist.

Back in the United States I was assigned to a Military Police unit at Sandia Base, New Mexico. The Army had an over-abundant supply of C.I.D. officers so I helped the MP's with security cracks. An identification badge, with the individual's picture on it, was required, to get into certain areas. If a person didn't have the right color and type of badge they would be denied entrance. My job was to see how effective the guards were in screening for those badges. I got into buildings with someone else's picture on it, with a woman's picture, a picture of an ape and even without a badge.

I did the job for two weeks. Then I was assigned as Documents Officer for the base. My days were busy, but my nights and weekends were free. I enrolled at the Albuquerque campus of the University of New Mexico. After transferring credits, and all the paperwork was done, I had one history course to take for a Bachelors of Arts in History. I challenged the course after a month.

With a Masters and a Bachelors Degree I had the notion that I was through with school. I knew I would continue to study, but in a different direction. I thought about geology. Something happened that put a stop to that idea.

First, I was RIF'd (Reduction in Force). I went to work one morning as a Captain and Documents Officer. I went home that night as a Corporal and a Documents Clerk. The Warrant Officer that used to work for me, was now my boss.

As documents clerk I joined an already full staff. This made the work very easy and gave me abundant free time. The Army was trying to decide what to do with me when something happened. There was a job that only I could accomplish.

I was called into a hastily assembled conference with several high-ranking officers, and some "suits", (men in business suits). One of the "suits" handed me a picture and asked if I knew the man in the picture. I said that I did, since it was a picture of me. He said, "No that is not your picture, that man is dead".

The "bird" colonel who was in charge told me about the man. He had worked with highly classified material while stationed in Korea. Just about the time he was to leave, to return to the United States, he died under very mysterious circumstances. He did not elaborate. One of the investigating officers had identified him as me.

Another one of the "suits" continued the story. "I happened to be there, not by accident. I confirmed that the dead man was, indeed, you. Now we need your help. We need to know about that man and what, if anything, was his involvement in the communist party. We need to know if he was involved in espionage. If he was, we need to know what he told the enemy".

The Colonel took over again. "I am authorized to offer you your commission back, permanently. But that is all. This is highly classified, illegal, and dangerous. It's strictly a volunteer mission. I can promise you some friendships in very high places, and preference on the promotion lists once you have completed the assignment and have you bars back.

The conference lasted for two hours. Most of that time was discussing the logistics. I agreed to the deception almost immediately. I am an American. My government needed me and I never questioned the assignment. I had been involved in much more dangerous ones, and just as illegal.

That night I was sent to Korea, by a fast jet, and loaded aboard a United States bound troop ship, as the other man. The other man had announced intentions of attending a Bible College in Springfield, Missouri, when he was discharged. I finished his "hitch" in the army and then went to school. I went to college full time and worked, just as he would have to have done. My Corporal's pay was as though he was drawing his tuition assistance from the G.I. Bill.

Once in the college I began to like it. I realized that, although I already had a degree in history, I had never studied the most important history. I never studied the history of the Christian Religion, or any other religion. This became my focus. The Bible became a history book. Archeology became the proof of the history recorded in the book. I thought I would like to have been an archeologist. He was going to become a preacher, so that was the course I took, but my interest was in the history of the various religious groups and, of course, the Bible's records.

No one ever questioned my identity. The man's parents lived several states away, so I encountered no problems from them. His wife was a shrew who hated him, so she didn't give me any problems either. I seldom dislike a person. She was an exception. Before he went into the Army they had had problems. His return didn't change matters as far as she was concerned. I never figured out why she stayed around. She certainly played around enough. She mentioned that I had changed one time. I told her that the Army does that to people, and she accepted it.

My time was spent in school, studying, and working. I got all of three or four hours of sleep a night. If it had not been for that woman I would have enjoyed every minute of the time. I reported my progress by "attending a preacher's conference" once in a while. I would leave town, make a telephone call, and meet someone at a designated location. At each reporting I requested relief, each time they told me to stay with it. Once I was able to make a final determination that the man had no involvement that would compromise the security of the country I had been in that school for over a year and a half. I had most of the credits earned, for a degree in Theology. I made my final report before another committee of Officers, and "suits".

There was a General Officer in charge of the final committee. He listened to my report, then complimented me on its thoroughness. Then he handed me my orders. I was to report to another base, as a Corporal, but would be promoted to Sergeant. That is when I mentioned that I was to be returned to the rank of Captain. This officer claimed that he knew nothing about that, and that it was just not possible. One word led to another. In the end he informed me that I was in the Army and I would do as I was "damn well told". I had had it! I informed the man that he had better take another look at my enlistment papers and my service record. I had over-stayed my enlistment my six months. I said something along the lines of, "I out rank you mister, I'm a civilian. I'm not even in your Army, and as long as you're in it I don't want to be a part of it". I did use a few more adjectives. I walked out. The General was sitting there with his mouth open and staring at my service record when I left. I never heard from the Army for a long time. When I did, it was to apologize. I decided the Military was not a career for me.

14.

I went back to the college and finished. After graduation, I discovered that the school was not accredited. Through one of the teachers I learned that there was a college in California that would accept most of my credits. It was accredited. I transferred to Western Baptist Bible College, and took another history course. After a couple weeks I challenged the course, and got my Bachelors of Theology. I still haven't figured out why I even wanted it, especially in another man's name.

Not long after receiving that diploma I was contacted by a government agency. The "suits" were able to "kill" the man I was impersonating. We faked a suicide and I returned to my original identity. The fact that I had been officially dead for a number of years didn't seem to bother them. I was informed that my service record was classified and only the President of the United States had access to the category. I got my Commission back. I was, once again, a Captain, but I chose to be in the inactive reserves. The bridge had been burned and I didn't want to rebuilt it. I was given a rather sizeable "mustering out" bonus, so I was not hurting for money.

I flew back to Texas, and Dallas, to make a new life. It didn't last long. I happened to run into an old aquaintance, from the Army. He was a captain in the infantry. He knew me from my old C.I.D. days and knew I was an investigator, so he hired me. He felt that his wife was cheating on him, and he wanted a divorce anyway. I was to prove that his premise was true. In that manner he could get his divorce, and she would get very little in the way of a settlement.

It was easy work. He filled me in on all the details I needed. She had a habit of stopping off at a little out-of-the-way private club, i.e. bar, after work, for a couple drinks. Sometimes she was two or three hours late getting home, because, "I got to talking to some of the girls". I met her at the bar. We talked for a while, then I left. After two meetings I asked her to accompany me to another club. She went, but on the way we decided to "go to my place".

I typed a full report and presented it to the Captain. I had been on the job less than a week. He paid me the two hundred and fifty he had promised, then read the report. That's when he decided to "thump on me" for sleeping with his wife. He didn't get far with the idea. I never saw him, or his wife, again. I heard that they got a divorce, and I was named as correspondent. She didn't contest it. I imagine she's still mad at me, but I'm sure he got over it. He recommended me to some friends.

I handled six divorce cases, in the Dallas area, then moved to California. A woman in Los Angeles contacted me. She said she got my name from a mutual friend, but didn't say who it was. She was about to marry her boss, and wanted him followed. The man had four ex-wives. It seems that he had a habit of marrying his private secretary. He would not allow his wife to work, so he hired another one, each time. He would become enamored with the new secretary and divorce his wife. This woman went to work for him with the express purpose of marrying, then divorcing him.

California was very generous with alimony payments at the time. She wanted to retire.

They were married less than three weeks, when he started playing around. A week later I had pictures of him, and his private secretary, in several very compromising poses. I had pictures of them "doin it", as the saying goes. It was easy. I just followed them out to their favorite picnic spot and used a telephoto lens, in broad daylight. My employer did retire. I got a sizeable bonus for being so quick. I flew back to Dallas for another case.

This case was different. I followed the couple to an old, run down, hotel. They still had keyholes in the doors. I waited until I was sure they were well along in their activities before I crept up to the door. My little camera was equipped with infrared film and had a "key hole attachment". I was about to start pushing the shutter when the door opened. The man was standing there with an Army 45 pointed at me. I did not check to see if it was loaded. I went across the hall, into a room, and out the window. I don't know if the room was occupied, or if the window was even open. I do know I dropped two stories and hit the sidewalk moving. I didn't see any point in being killed over a "stupid divorce".

Less than a block from the hotel the pain got to me. I had crushed the cartilage in both ankles, and both knees. I could hardly walk. I hailed a cab and went home. I sat for two hours, thinking. I decided to get out of the detective business and out of Dallas. I called a friend and gave away both of my cars, my book collection, and everything else. I gathered all the money I had around and had her take me to the airport. I took a flight to Seattle. It took some time to heal up from my leg injures but eventually I could walk without hurting.

Life got routine after that. I say I actually became a regular human being, with some minor exceptions which I will tell about in another story. I've named that one *Flyswatter*—for a very good reason.

FLYSWATTER

by

George Wright

for Geri

This story is based on the true events of my life. I took some liberties to make it more interesting but only a few. I submit this as fiction because of that and because no one is going to believe it anyway.

1.

Just before five in the early hours of morning is no time to be calling me. The ring sounded far away, at first, and then it sounded like a train had entered the room. I was still groggy from sleep, but I had an idea who might be on the other end of the line. After fumbling around to find a light switch on the bedside lamp I picked up the receiver. My voice sounded like I had a hangover as I said, "This better be important". I heard several tones beating out a rhythm. My response was automatic.

I was, suddenly, fully alert as I responded by pressing several buttons in reply. I was being called out again. My premonition was right. At such an early hour it had to be a wrong number, or the government. The particular office, for which I occasionally worked, had absolutely no conception of time, or time zones. It was almost 9 a.m. in Washington DC, so they assumed that everyone in the nation was awake.

A word here and there, with a few more beeps, told me to go to Boeing Field. An airplane would be waiting for me. I knew the routine. Once we were in the air the pilot would hand me sealed orders. I put the coffee on to cook and got cleaned up. After a quick cup of the wake-up fluid and some cold meat I walked out of my door, as though I was going to the office; just as thousands of other men all over Seattle would be doing, in two or three more hours. I wore a suit, and carried a briefcase. Instead of papers, the case contained the necessities of an overnight trip.

I reflected back over the years as I drove - back to the beginning. It was the first time I had ever done that, but it was also the first time I had ever considered quitting. It was the first time the telephone call was not welcome. I was considering marriage to a young lady who would never understand my unique sideline, even if I could tell her about it. She certainly would not condone my sudden disappearances for periods of time, at least the last wife didn't. She kicked me out after only nine months.

It all started when I was an army officer in the C.I.D. (Criminal Investigation Department). I was stationed in Pusan, Korea when my government "discovered" me, and I found out a few things about myself. An unknown, but very efficient, department in the Army under the direct command of the Commander In Chief decided I fulfilled their perquisites for a special kind of soldier.

I am an orphan. I was left on a doorstep at a very young age. The folks who raised me, until I was nine, died. I was alone, with no close ties to friends, or family. I was free to travel at a moment's notice and almost no one would miss me. There were other, more deeply rooted, reasons why I was the person they wanted.

By nature, the human being is a social creature. Beginning with birth, attachments are formed which mold the individual and largely determine what kind of person he, or she, will become in the future. It is called "love", "family", or "bonding" and takes place in the first four or five years of life. When this process is interrupted by death, divorce, or other traumatic events, it usually begins all over again. Interrupt the same process enough times and the attachments are never made. The person is never completed. In any event, we humans are largely a product of our environment.

In my case, the formative process was interrupted so many times that I had subconsciously learned not to become attached to any other human being. For every action there is an equal and opposite reaction. By learning not to become attached to people, one learns not to be compassionate. It can become as easy to take a human life, as it is to kill an animal - even easier.

Yet, every human being will "bond" to someone, or something. Sometimes it is a church, or philosophy. At times it is an ideal.

On some occasions this bonding is to the nation. When patriotic people consistently influence a very young person there is a tenancy to become dedicated to the nation, in much the same was as most youngsters "worship" parents, or the family. I happen to have been one of those people. The only truly consistent thing in my young life was the patriotism of authority figures.

Other factors came into play as well. I was selected because I fit other qualifications. A very good marksman, both with a rifle and with a pistol, An IQ high enough to make me a "quick study" (I learn quickly), fiercely patriotic, no close friends, wife, or relatives, and no compunctions about following orders without question. I had one other qualification that made me particularly desirable. I am the kind of person that is never noticed. There is nothing physical that makes me stick in the mind; I am not out-going or pushy. I am the one that no one bothers about. No one notices when I am at the party, or if left two hours ago.

I certainly don't look like the stereotype of an agent for the government.

The last qualification is one that gets complicated. They needed men who could kill without conscience. Killing another human being in combat, during a war, is somewhat different. Not that there is not an amount of trauma. Soldiers experience trauma when they first get into combat, but in war, the killing is done mostly in self-defense.

In the line of duty this is not always true. Sometimes you are protecting another person's life, or property. At other times it may be to keep a felon from getting away. There are psychoanalysts that can help both the soldier and the one who kills in the line of duty, be it a police officer or someone else. There is a healing process that will help almost every patient.

People who have killed in the "heat of the moment", or accidentally, can get counseling to help them. Criminals that kill without conscience are locked up, or executed, for their actions. Psychopaths kill for fun, or from compulsion. These people are judged insane and locked up, or executed.

There is another kind of person who is capable of killing other people. The individual is generally a male. He is familiar with guns, and is a hunter. He possesses a very strong sense of right and wrong, and is honest in dealing with the law, and others. He has no fear of death, but he is neither careless nor reckless. There seems to be an acceptance that he will eventually die and he is reconciled to his fate. As a rule, he likes strategy games, like chess, and is mild mannered. The ideal age is between 18 and 35. After he is about thirty or thirty-five he has, generally, taken on some responsibilities. He begins to value his life. Most people who have these attributes live their entire lives without knowing. They live a very normal life.

A very small number of these people learn about their special talent and use it. Always, they learn by accident. Most of those who use the ability never reach thirty years of age and very few people notice their passing. One out of a thousand of them live to enjoy their senior years. As a rule the deeds of their youth haunt them.

Political, and domestic, turmoil seem to bring out this kind of person. In some areas of the world, these are the patriots that begin revolutions. In the United States, and other stable countries, they remain dormant. A trauma can bring them forth. There has been a series of movies about just such an individual. A personal tragedy causes the man to take revenge when the police can't help him. He becomes a vigilante and cleans up the streets by killing the bad guys. He never gets caught, or rather prosecuted. At the end of the movie he is asked to leave town.

2.

I was just leaving Queen Anne Hill, when I thought back to the incident that started it all. My talent was discovered quite by accident. The United States Army found out about it for me. Someone in the Army told someone else, who wrote a report and the report, was sent out. Someone saw that report and I was pointed in the direction they wanted me to go. I spent 43 years going in that direction from time to time.

There are times when events just seem to happen. We do our jobs as best we can and circumstances seem to happen without any control. I guess you could call it fate or coincidence but I think of it more as the luck of the draw. This time we drew two cards to a royal flush. It happened in Korea not too long after the end of the Korean Conflict.

The Korean C.I.D. had notified us that there seemed to be a larger than normal amount of American goods on the black market. Service men had a habit of buying things at the post exchange and selling them on the street, especially cigarettes. Although not legal the offence had always been overlooked unless blatant. What was happening was a flooding of the market, of PX merchandise. Truckloads of American army stores had to have been sold.

At the time I was the Officer in Charge of a two man team. Our specialty was auditing records. We were ordered to conduct audits of several warehouses in the

Pusan area; in an effort to discover whither the goods were coming from the U.S. Army.

The team consisted of M/Sgt. Corbin, a career man with eighteen years in the army and me. To look at him one would picture a bricklayer, or a construction laborer, but when he spoke you might think more of a college professor. He had taken courses in accounting through correspondence and knew exactly what to look for. Corbin was just Corbin to everyone who knew him. Few people had ever heard his first name.

My master's degree is in business, with a specialty in accounting and auditing. I looked the part, horned rim glasses and all, of an absolute nerd. I am the kind of person no one ever really sees in a crowd. If you wanted my name you had to look in my records. They all called me GI because of my initials, and because a "GI" was the very last thing anyone would describe me as being.

We were teamed together when we first arrived in Korea. Actually we had both been on the same ship from the States. We became friends during the trip because of a mutual interest in Chess. I had the Ration Breakdown detail for the troop ship and Corbin was my Sergeant. Our job was to requisition the day's food from the hold. Eight enlisted men would pull the supplies and deliver them to the mess, - or galley. Corbin and I spent the rest of the day playing chess, and eating fig Newton's with ice cream.

We walked into headquarters together, and were given the assignment as a team of experts. We thought of it as a "gravy job". We could avoid any of the hard criminal activity and take it easy.

The investigation netted nothing for almost three months. Then 83 days into the project we started on the second to the last warehouse. The second day into the audit I noticed that there were more than, what would be considered, normal shipments to one post exchange, and all signed by a M/Sgt Davids. We decided to check the location personally just to see if the shipments were authorized. Two hours later and almost thirty miles north of Pusan we arrived at our destination. We expected to find a large base with an equally large exchange. We were in for a little surprise.

It was an old army ordinance depot that had been vacated since the signing of the ceasefire. The few buildings that were left were deserted except for the rats. Weeds grew everywhere, and there was a sign posted by the government of Korea that read, "No Trespassing" in Korean, and English. We saw tracks left by trucks entering and leaving and noticed a fairly new padlock securing the gate.

When we returned to the office we had our usual progress reports typed and sent to headquarters. For the next three days we continued with our investigation gathering more information as to specifically what was shipped to that base and how much of each item.

We also started a check of the service records of all the men working at the warehouse. At 0800 hours on the fourth day I received a telephone call from headquarters telling me to pick up M/Sgt Davids. Written orders would follow. It looked like we nailed one by auditing the books. At 0810 hours we received the requested service records. Something did not ring true.

M/Sgt Davids was a veteran of 19 years with an outstanding record. He was wounded in the last days of WWII and again in the Korean conflict. Both Corbin and I felt Davids should be given the benefit of the doubt and further investigation was required. We felt, with his record, Davids could not have been so dishonest. Two Purple Hearts, a Silver Star, several letters of commendation and 19 years just don't add up to a crook. I told headquarters we still had some evidence to collect and it would take another three or four days. In order to have a Court Martial in the Army, the evidence must be very good so headquarters agreed.

We continued to investigate. We hung around the warehouse looking at first one record and then another, gathering volumes of material, and getting the routine of the place. In the next three days we had a complete record including dates, amounts and items that were stolen. All that remained was a check of the dates the various personnel were assigned to the warehouse. Anyone assigned there after the thefts started would be a poor suspect.

It came as no surprise to discover there were no shipments to the old ordinance depot and everyone was the picture of efficiency from the beginning of the audit. Twenty-seven men worked there counting the Officer in Charge, Lt. Kawadakowski, M/Sgt Davids, Cpl. Koch and 24 privates. Lt. Kawadakowski and M/Sgt Davids were the only ones authorized to sign outgoing invoices and approve requisitions.

Lt. Kawadakowski was a college man who got his commission through the R.O.T.C. program. He was not married and was somewhat of a playboy. We discovered that he had seldom been at his post and was spending a lot of time with his Korean girlfriend. Other than that, the Lieutenant seemed clean but derelict in his duties. It began to look more and more as though Davids was our man. Pressure was building up to do something. Headquarters began to think we were dragging our feet. The investigation had taken 105 days and that was too long.

Word was passed down from my good friend, the clerk typist at the Far East Command Headquarters in Japan. "The General got hold of this and wants action". I had a Major for a boss. The Major's boss was a "Bird" Colonel and his boss was the General. General Locke was in charge of all C.I.D. operations in the Far East and had a reputation for being a thorough investigator that demanded complete documentation and conclusive evidence before any action could be taken. My clerk typist friend informed me that I had until Monday or Tuesday since he had learned directly from General Locke's office and written orders were coming through channels.

It was a cold Friday night in November. Not being much of a sleeper anyway, and bothered about the investigation, I decided to go for a long walk just to think about things. You could not call it "taking the night air" since at that time Pusan was the largest city in the world without a sewer system. This activity was nothing unusual as I often went for walks late at night after the city calmed down, and the streets were more or less deserted.

I had a friend named Lee who was a Korean police officer on night patrol. We had met and talked from time to time when I was out walking. I hoped to run into him and talk about the Korean black market.

My travels took me from Pier 1 up through Pusan proper until I found myself, at 0230, in an area off limits to military personnel. This didn't worry me as I had been here several times before. The main street wasn't dangerous but the side streets definitely were. Many soldiers had lost their money, and sometimes their lives in this area. I was armed and, because of my position in the C.I.D., authorized to be there.

Just as I started to pass a narrow street known, for obviously good reasons, by every American Soldier as Gonorrhea Alley I heard scuffling and an American voice calling for help. "Oh Great!" another soldier wandered off to where he shouldn't be and is getting rolled. Will those guys ever learn there is a reason this place is off limits", I thought.

The street is about twenty feet wide, and lighted only by the lights from the windows of several Whore Houses along the way. Not knowing what I was getting into I drew my weapon and stepped into the street. Someone had to pull that idiot's fat out of the fire! I stepped around a pile of baskets, with gun in hand, to see, about 25 feet away, a soldier on the ground with two big Koreans over him. There was the flash of steel. They had some very wicked looking knives and were about to strike. That poor fool was as good as dead!

The first shot from my 38 special took one Korean just behind the left ear. He dropped like a falling tree right on top of the hapless man on the ground. The noise, and the sudden fall of the first man, took the second by surprise. He looked up just in time to take the second round between the eyes about an inch up from the eyebrows. The impact threw him against the wall of a building. He slid down the wall, and his dead body sat there like a passed-out drunk.

Seconds later I was rolling the dead Korean off the poor "slob" on the ground. "You alright"? I said, as I helped the man up, and gathered my thoughts, to give him a royal ass chewing for being there in the first place. Then I was going to call the Military Police. As I helped him up the reflection of the lighted windows showed a single star on the shoulder of the "fool".

All thought of chewing out this man vanished with amazement. "What is a General doing here this time of night?" All I could manage to choke out was, "get your ass out of here fast!" Without a word, the General left in a hurry. What he was doing there, or who he was, or where he went, I never even wanted to know. The report went in as an unidentified American serviceman. The General could not have known who saved him that night. C.I.D. personnel wore only an olive green uniform with no insignia other than two US buttons, no designation of rank and no nametag.

That ended my Friday night walk, or better yet, Saturday morning very early. By the time I finished typing the shooting report it was just after o-four hundred hours. I slept soundly for three hours before Corbin was pounding on my door. Over breakfast we talked about the shooting, but I never mentioned the General. We went back to the office to discuss the investigation.

Reluctantly, we decided there was no choice other than to charge M/Sgt Davids. The clerk typist started on the papers. It would take him a long time because of the regulations. There can be no errors, strikeovers, or erases on court martial papers. Even though it was Saturday afternoon we decided to get things started and have it done by Monday morning. It's not a good idea to make all your bosses mad - all the way up to the Far East Commander. Orders were coming, within the next two days, and we wanted the jump on them.

It was Sunday, and the paperwork was almost done when a telephone call came in. There was a fire at the warehouse! The O.I.C. (Officer in Charge) at the fire department thought it prudent to call when he noticed a strong gasoline smell, even though there was no gasoline stored near the warehouse. On the way over we decided it would be a good idea to pick up Lt. Kawadakowski. He was not in, probably with his girl, or at the Officers Club.

We went to M/Sgt Davids' barracks but were informed that he was in town somewhere so we proceeded toward the warehouse. About four blocks from the warehouse we noticed Cpl. Koch. Koch did not seem too happy to see two C.I.D. investigators when the jeep stopped, probably because he reeked of gasoline.

Corbin had a habit of always carrying a small tape recorder. He turned it on as I ordered Koch into the jeep. It only took one breath to smell the fuel. I asked, "Well Corporal why did you start a fire at the warehouse?" He said, "What fire?" Corbin said, "The one you started! You are four blocks away, and going away from the biggest fire you've ever seen. You smell of gas and smoke. Answer the Lieutenant!" When a Master Sergeant that looks like he could eat you for breakfast asks a question in the tone of voice Corbin used there are usually results.

At this point there was no proof of arson, or of Cpl. Koch's involvement in arson, but assumption sometimes pays off. Koch confessed. He said, "Alright I did it". By this time we had arrived at the fire.

Corbin asked the big question. Why?

The answer startled both of us. "Because you were getting too close."

A glance showed that the recorder was still recording. We showed no emotion. "As a matter of fact we were just preparing the papers for a Court Martial" said Corbin, not bothering to say who the papers would charge.

I said, "Why don't you just tell us all about it, beginning with why you started stealing and ending with this fire."

Cpl. Koch joined the Army to keep from going to jail. A Judge in the Midwest ordered him to enlist in hopes that the Army could do what parents and civilian government could not. He had an arrest record going back to when he was 10 years old, mostly petty theft. In the Army he was suspected in three different cases but never charged. He had been in the service for 27 months when assigned to the warehouse detail. Promoted to Corporal because of time in grade and to fill a vacancy he found himself in a good position. All he had to do was to learn the routine, study Davids' signature and set up his distribution system.

He started with just a few items that he carried out himself until he contacted a Korean with access to an Army vehicle from during the conflict. The Korean informed him that he and his associates would take all they could get. The Korean was the one who came up with the old ordinance depot. When his big break in the black market came, Cpl. Koch was using M/Sgt Davids' name and was wearing the proper clothing. The gang of Korean criminals thought they were doing business with Davids.

Business started booming! Koch typed phony requisitions, shipped merchandise to his phony ordinance depot and signed M/Sgt Davids' name to every one of them. He told us he knew it could have been proved that Davids had not signed some of the shipping orders and that would prove he was guilty. Shipments were made when Davids was in Japan on R & R (Rest and Recuperation). When we pulled those particular records he thought his luck had run out.

We had not discovered this piece of evidence. To cover his tracks he went to the warehouse, dumped all the records in the middle of the floor and doused them with gasoline. He then fashioned a wick out of gas by pouring a fine trail of gas all the way out the doors. He started it on fire and left the building.

If he had not stayed to watch from across the street, and ran into us, he probably would have gotten away for a while longer. He knew M/Sgt Davids was not in the barracks and would not be able to account for his whereabouts. He had slipped the Sergeant a "Mickey", and he was sleeping it off in the bedroom of Koch's whore. He thought he had succeeded in destroying everything. All records, the warehouse and its contents; over half of a million dollars was destroyed by the arson.

He evidently didn't know we had a lot of the records in our briefcases and had taken them to study in my quarters. The evidence we needed to back up his confession was still intact.

The prisoner deposited with the Military Police, we went back to the office and rewrote the report and court martial papers. The clerk typist had finished his job and had gone when we arrived. We waited until Monday morning to give him the news. He would have to start all over again.

On Monday morning I called my boss, the major, and gave an oral report. The typewritten report was sent through channels to the Far East Commander. We took the rest of the day to celebrate.

One week later I was a Captain. Master Sergeant Corbin went from E-7 to E-8. The incident in the alley was never investigated, and all records disappeared. The warehouse case was blown all out of proportion, which resulted in promotions long before they were due. Two C.I.D. investigators decided not to argue with the results.

We were presented to the President of Korea and given a medal for our work. Big deal! It was the same Unit Citation medal he gave it to all servicemen who served in Korea.

Cpl. Koch got forty years for Arson, theft of government property, forgery, profiteering on the black market and various other charges. M/Sgt Davids got a reprimand, and a transfer, for not keeping an eye on things. Lt. Kwiatkowski was also reprimanded, and charged with conduct unbecoming of an officer. He kept his job and lost his girlfriend. The Koreans involved were all rounded up by the Korean C.I.D.. No one knows what happened, but most of them, and a couple government officials, were found dead by various means and under various circumstances.

Five years after leaving the service I got "the rest of the story". An old friend from Korea, Mr. Lee, happened to be in Seattle at a Police Chief's convention. We met, by chance, in one of the better "watering holes" one evening and I told him my side of the Gonorrhea Alley incident. He gave me the missing pieces. General Locke had contacted him and told his story. Lee gave my name as the one who would have been in the area at the time of the incident. When I made out the shooting incident report the General knew.

General Locke had decided to do some investigation on his own. He decided to approach the case from the other end so the entire operation could be stopped. He arranged a meeting with the head of the Korean C.I.D., the Chief of Police and the Mayor of Pusan. They agreed to meet him at a secret place in downtown Pusan. At the meeting the Korean C.I.D. man introduced him to Mr. Lee, the Chief of Police, and Mr. Kim Ling, the Mayor of Pusan.

Two informants were brought in. They told General Locke that the contact in the military was M/Sgt Davids. They gave details that were confirmed by Lee and Ling as being fact. The meeting started at 2300 hours and was not ended until nearly 0230 the following morning. General Locke had all the proof he needed as he left the meeting on that cold November morning in downtown Pusan. First thing Monday morning he would throw M/Sgt. Davids in the guardhouse, and read the riot act to a couple C.I.D. investigators.

He was just leaving his meeting place when he was approached by the two informants he had met earlier. Thinking they had something else to tell him he greeted them warmly - then they attacked. He fought them off until he stumbled on a protruding piece of cobblestone and went down. Involuntarily he called for help! Someone started shooting. One of the Koreans fell on top of him and the other was thrown against a building. A couple seconds later he was being helped up. His rescuer asked, "You OK?", but before he could answer he heard a gasp and then, "get your ass out of here."

3.

A couple months after the incident in the alley I was ordered to undergo an "evaluation". After two weeks of endless hours of interviews, and tests, I was offered a job. I was told that I could be of great service to the United States and I was uniquely qualified for a special project. The officer who interviewed me told me his name was Jim and I had no need to know anything else about him. He could not, or would not, tell me the nature of my new assignment. He said I would find out in due time. Telling me I would be a great service to the nation did it for me. He had hit my "hot button". I volunteered.

I was put on TDY (Temporary Duty) and sent to one of the offshore islands near Pusan, for training. I had thought the "evaluation" was ordered because I had shown no emotional upset over having to shoot two people. I had thought I might be in trouble. I guess I was, but not the way I thought.

There were six other men being trained. For the next three months we learned the fine art of assassination. Our boss was Jim. All we had were initials. Discussing anything outside of training was forbidden. None of us have ever known another's name, occupation, or hometown. By keeping my mouth shut, and my ears open, I learned that there were only two other military men in the group, and all of us had killed one, or more, times. At the end of training, everyone was returned to their regular jobs, except me.

My attention was drawn back to the present. I had arrived at Boeing Field in south Seattle. Exactly fifty-nine minutes after the telephone so rudely interrupted my sleep, I walked up to a Lear jet and asked an anxious looking pilot, "You looking for a rider?"

"Only if you're going my way", he replied.

So far, so good! I gave the prescribed reply, "If Jim says I'm going your way, I guess I'm flying." Five minutes later we had cleared the field and turned south. I could see the sun reflecting off Mt. Rainier as it prepared for another day. It was a Saturday morning, so I was not worried about loosing another job, not yet. If I was gone more than two days I would have to make up a reasonable excuse, or find a new position. That would be nothing new. This little hobby of mine had put me on the list of the unemployed several times. Bosses don't take kindly to employees that disappear for three, or four, days at a time. I found out that girl friends don't like it either.

This would be mission number twenty-seven, but only the third in five years. The first twenty-four took place during the first five years after training. Thinking about that got me to reflecting on my life once more.

After that one "big case" that ended with a warehouse fire my regular duty assignments were lessened. I spent so much time on "Special Duty" or "TDY" that nearly all the work was done by Sergeant Corbin. He didn't mind. He rather liked working alone, with me as a consultant. In a fifteen month period I was called upon twenty one times, to take care of a "problem". Most jobs took only two or three days, but several were much more complicated.

121

Immediately after my initial training my TDY was extended and I was flown to Japan, where I was transferred to a private aircraft. Everything I needed was on board. I changed from the plain OD uniform, to civilian clothes and reviewed the sealed orders that the pilot handed me. Someone was going to have a fatal accident.

I knew I was under a microscope. This first assignment went so smooth it surprised me. The big secret in my line of work is speed. Get in, get it done, and get out. The first mission was just that quick. The information I was given on the subject looked good. He lived high on a mountainside, the road leading to his place went along one side of a canyon. The drop to the bottom, at one particular hairpin turn, was over a hundred feet. I decided to use that curve. Orders said the man had to have an accident. The nice thing about that curve was that anyone driving down the canyon would not be able to see around the corner of the cliff. Anything on the road would cause a problem. Obviously, it was a very dangerous part of the road.

He had been watched as he drove down that road precisely at 0805. He left his garage at 0800 every morning, five days a week. On Sundays he left two hours earlier for early services at his church. During the day I played tourist, complete with sunglasses, loud shirt, shorts, and camera. While wandering around I was looking for something that I could use. In the industrial section of the city I found what I needed, a two and a half ton dump truck. It would be parked, at least for the night, and ready for my unauthorized use.

I spent the next seven hours being seen, but not being a spectacle. I was just another foreigner on holiday. At 3 a.m. (0300 hours) I slipped away from the cocktail lounge at one of the better hotels. If anyone noticed my departure, they would have thought I was only going to my room. In fact, I never had a room, but the bartender and waitress both thought I did. Both of them asked if I wanted to put my drinks on my hotel bill, but I graciously declined.

The truck I had spotted earlier was still there, with four others that had been left later. I hot-wired one, and drove away. At 0500 hours the truck was crossways in the road just around the hairpin curve. As the subject came speeding along the road, and rounded the curve, he slammed on his brakes and turned the wheel. I had thought it would be necessary to push his car over the precipice, but his panicked action saved a lot of trouble. The car spun around on the dew dampened pavement and went right over the cliff.

There was no fire, or explosion, but when I looked down I could see gasoline leaking from a ruptured tank. There was a coil of rope inside the dump truck. I cut off a section about three feet long and stuck the end of it deep into the truck's gas tank. Back at the edge of the cliff, I lit the rope and flipped it down so that it landed on the wrecked vehicle. The fire, and explosion, followed within seconds, but not before I spotted the man. He was still sitting in the driver's seat. He was probably already dead, but now I knew for sure.

Two hours later the truck was right back where I had gotten it and I was boarding an airplane. By the time the "accident" was discovered I was on the way back to my bunk in Korea. As far as I know no one ever suspected foul play in the death of one highly placed government official in the Philippines, whose sideline was selling secrets to China.

Because that one individual sought to protect himself from his peers by leaving a letter behind that read, "In case of my sudden demise . . . " Three agents inside the United States, two in Great Britain, and one in France were arrested. The Chinese lost one of their major sources of information.

Under normal conditions I would never know the who, or why, of a job. This time I found out through a friend. I was told about the events that followed the "accident" by a friend in the CIC (Counter Intelligence Corps). My friend laughed at how ironic it was that an auto accident had proven so useful to the United States Government. I didn't tell him that the very existence of the letter he left behind, was the reason for the man's death. His insurance policy had become his death warrant.

4.

I spent two weeks doing very little. I caught up on some correspondence courses I had taken, and relaxed. I helped on an investigation, but only for a few hours. It soon became time for another "TDY".

The target was a man with habits. He would be at the same place, at the same time, every day. His routine was so rigid that one could set a clock by his appearance. It was easy to find an isolated location, and set up the shot.

The location I picked was very public, but on the border of a run-down section of the city. It was the only time I could get a clear field of vision, without any interference. There happened to be an abandoned building about a block away. I discovered that I could enter the structure through an unlocked door and reach the sixth floor without attracting attention. It was a good spot.

No one really noticed the non-descript, typical tourist. He was dressed just like all of the others. He was of medium height, medium build, and regular brown hair, nothing distinctive. He was one of those many people one sees, but doesn't see. No one made any connection to the sightseer with the over-sized camera bag that took way too many pictures.

During the day someone shot, and killed, a local celebrity. The man was shot through the head by a small caliber bullet and died before he hit the ground. No one even heard the shot. It was not until later that they determined from where the shot was fired, and even then it was only a scientific guess. They figured the angle, and direction, of entry and decided it came from the roof of a building about a block away.

There were a few errors in their "scientific guess". The man turned, about ninety degrees, when he fell. They had the wrong direction, and the wrong building. I didn't think it would be a good idea to correct them.

The picture taking tourist was at the scene. He was questioned briefly, but when he said he had just arrived, and someone confirmed his statement, the police quickly forgot about him.

"Nondescript", a most valuable asset, caused me to not be noticed in a number of other countries. Over a period of time I appeared, but was not seen, in seventeen different countries. In each, someone died. The causes varied, but death is still death. To my knowledge no connection was ever made between the events.

I was flown directly from that job to the third one. It took a few hours to get there, so I knew I was in another country, in another part of the world. After I got off the airplane, I was transferred to a helicopter and flown deep into a mountainous area. My orders were to wait near a road in the foothills until my target arrived. The road was two tracks of dirt, where vehicles had passed through and made a country lane.

My first clue, as to the duration of the job, was when the pilot helped me unload food and a sleeping bag. He seemed to think that I was a privileged civilian who wanted to "rough it" for a few days. There was a good stream and the gear included fishing equipment. I set up camp and began to enjoy my "outing". The pilot said he would be back in five days, to get me.

The road was so rough that there would be no chance of hitting a target, or even the car, without a lot of luck, and risk. To eliminate this factor I went to work. The camping gear included a small shovel, a military type entrenching tool, used for digging foxholes.

The spot I was looking for turned out to be nearly a half-mile from my campsite. The road went between two hills, with the stream running between them. The gully was wooded but the hills were only sparsely treed. On the one hill I could see a number of rocks, which could be dislodged. The other hill one offered a place of concealment between two large boulders.

It didn't take long to create a rockslide that blocked the road. It took longer to cross over and find the right spot for the shot. I was fortunate. My campsite was in a position that afforded me a view of the road as it wound its way along. I would be able to see the vehicle in plenty of time to get into position.

I waited, and waited. Three days later I saw a pickup truck with a canopy approaching. The scope on my rifle picked out the driver, and passenger. The passenger was my target. The driver was a bodyguard, or a chauffer. The truck was moving faster than good sense would dictate, so I had to hurry. I made it to my "shooting platform" only seconds before the car stopped at the slide.

The driver got out and started moving rocks. I thought I would have to risk a shot through the side window, but the passenger decided to stretch his legs. He stood back watching his driver work. He was not about to help.

The target had his arms raised, stretching. And his mouth was open, in a yawn, when he died. The slug entered the left side of his head, and exited the right. He seemed frozen in place for a moment, then dropped to the ground.

The driver never noticed. He was bending down, struggling with a large rock, when the back of his head was fragmented by my second round.

I went to the pickup, made sure they were both dead, and loaded them back into their respective seats. Then I started the engine and headed the vehicle toward the ditch. It wound up at the bottom of the gully, next to the creek. Then I punctured the gas tank and started the truck on fire. Afterward, I went back to camp.

I decided to try my luck with the fishing pole. I dined on fish that evening. The next morning I packed my gear and went fishing again while I waited for my ride back to civilization. When the pilot saw my catch he commented that my camping trip must have been successful. I agreed.

Some jobs are easier than others. The first one was rather quick and easy, thanks to some luck and good surveillance earlier. The only complication was that it had to be an accident, or natural causes. The next two were, more or less, simple assassinations with a long-range rifle. When I was being briefed for the fourth job, I mentioned the fact that all of the other missions had been easy and that I felt anyone could have completed the job without my help.

That is when Jim explained, "It takes time to do the profile. The people doing that become recognizable, or even known. We have to get those people out. Every mission has people of various talents. Whenever we try to cross over to another area of expertise with an individual, the job gets loused up and months of work are lost. When your mission succeeds, it is because of the work that has already been done. There are only seven people like you. It is you seven that complete the job for those who start it. Did you ever think that those jobs were easy because you're damn good at your job?"

5.

The fourth job was different. It had to be an obvious murder that could be blamed on a particular party. It got complicated.

I was taken by boat to Japan, where I was briefed and then shuttled off to an airplane. Hours later I transferred to a small single engine craft and flown out after dark. We flew low to avoid radar detection. Even in the darkness I could see trees, and the shimmering of water in the streams. I saw hills looming above us several times. Eventually, we landed in a field.

It was not an inhabited area, but there was an old dirt road. The road was the only sign that human beings had ever been to the area. My next mode of transportation would be the motor scooter the pilot hauled out of the cargo bay, along with my gear and my weapon. It was a very high-powered rifle, with a special scope and a silencer. The slug this weapon fires is small, but it is extremely accurate up to five thousand yards.

The aerial photographs, and the map, I was given at the briefing showed a trail leading directly west. I traveled until nearly noon before I stopped to rest. I hid the scooter under some branches and leaves, then lay down to sleep until dark. I was still nearly two and a half miles from my tentative destination, but I would be in a patrolled area soon.

Before sleeping, I studied the maps, photographs, and my instructions. All I knew was that there were two "villas" east of a large city. The houses were over a mile apart, with a high hill about halfway between them. I was told that they were the homes of two feuding crime lords. I suspected they were drug dealers, but I was not told. Tension had been mounting between them for some time, but recent events made it look as though they were about to unify. Something was needed to stop their peace negotiations and set them against each other again. A war between the rival gangs could eradicate as many as two hundred gangsters. As the voice behind the screen at the briefing said, "Their government has asked for our help. Officially we can't do a thing for them, but it is in our own best interests that this war start".

I was approaching my objective, that hill separating the two villas. I came in from the back. Reconnaissance had shown patrols from both sides and their patrol areas. None of them patrolled the top of the hill. I was, obviously, considered too far away and neutral territory. It made a good barrier between the two differing patrols. I knew there had been no incursions from one camp to the other in several months, not since the negotiations for a truce had started. The men on patrol would have relaxed their vigilance. Still, I wanted the cover of darkness, just in case. I memorized as much as I could from the map and started up the trail. I had walked about a mile when I heard two men talking as they walked. I had met the first patrol. They walked within ten feet of my hiding place, behind some bushes.

I knew I was on the south side of the hill so I started angling off to my right, up hill. It was slow going because I was not anxious to make any more noise than necessary. When the moon come out I had just reached the crest. This made moving easier and with much better vision, but the patrols could see better as well. I stayed away from the crest of the hill so as to not form a silhouette from either side.

The hill was actually a long "hog back" about three quarters of a mile in length. I worked my way along until I spotted lights from the house to my left. A few steps further, and I saw the one on the right. When it looked as though I was positioned directly between the two, I stopped. The top of the hog back, at this point, was strewn with boulders, most of then five or six feet in diameter. I selected one, and sighted through the riflescope at the villas to my left. I could see everything I wanted. A few feet away, I found my spot for the one on the other side. The view was terrific. Now it was time to rest until daylight. I was not going to get a shot until morning.

The sun woke me by shining in my face. Both buildings were still in the shadows, so I waited. About nine o'clock I was checking the targets when I heard shooting near by. My heart was in my throat before I investigated. Not a hundred yards down the hill three men were shooting pistols at something. My scope revealed a paper target about a hundred feet away from the gunmen. When I focused on the target I noticed that not one of them had even hit the paper. By ten the target shooters had moved on. A quick check of my surroundings revealed no one within a hundred to a hundred fifty yards of my position. I prepared for my day's work.

The range finder built into the scope revealed that the one dwelling was seventeen hundred and thirty one yards, to the sliding glass doors on the patio. The other building was eighteen hundred and ten yards to a similar spot. I was thinking how similar the two buildings were, when a man walked right into my sights. He sat at a patio table while two other men started serving him his breakfast. I went over to look at the other villa. A man was standing in the threshold of the now open glass doors. A servant handed him a cup of coffee. I had recognized both men from the pictures I had been given, and had in my shirt pocket.

Adjusting for windage, I aimed about three inches to one side of the center of his forehead. There was no need to adjust for the drop of the bullet. My scope made that adjustment for me. A squeezed the trigger and watched through the scope as the slug entered his left eye. The back of the coffee drinker's head burst apart as the projectile slammed against the inside of his skull and passed on through.

Before anyone in that villa could act, I was taking aim at the man eating his breakfast in the other villa. My man was lazily eating, and talking to a female companion. My adjustment for windage was more accurate this time. Again, I heard the soft pop of the silencer equipped rifle and watched as the slug entered the man's temple, right on target. The lead evidently rattled around inside of the skull, because it exited just under his chin. The woman jumped up, to reveal some interesting body parts. I had not noticed earlier, that she was nude. I thought it was too bad I didn't have time to enjoy the scenery.

As soon as they discovered the direction from which the bullets came, the hill would be infested with angry patrols, from both sides. They would, in all likelihood, blame each other for the death of their leaders. At first, they would not know about both killings, only that of their own man.

It would be a bloody mess. I would be in the middle of a battlefield. The thought of either side finding me was not comforting. Leaving the hill in broad daylight would be a sure ticket to the cemetery, but staying would likely have the same result. My best hope was to get out of there fast. I made it nearly a half-mile when I was forced to find a "hidey hole" and wait for dark.

The brush was particularly thick at the base of a huge rock. I could see a path, made by some kind of animal, into that thicket. I crawled in, doing my best to cover up any scuffmarks I had made. Once inside the thicket, I discovered a hollowed out place at the base of the rock. The overhang had served as a den for some animal. I thought, from the tracks, it had to be a member of the canine family. Since I didn't even know what continent I was on, let alone what country I was in, I had no idea exactly what animal had reared its young there. I did know it would be my refuge, since the men I had heard thrashing through the brush were now at the thicket. They paused only a moment, and ran off.

I rolled in the dirt until I was covered with dust, and would blend with my surroundings. Other than getting as far into the den as possible, and remaining very quiet, there was nothing more for me to do, but wait for darkness. Darkness would be a while getting there, but I didn't have to wait long for the start of excitement.

Several men were within thirty feet of my place of concealment when they were fired upon by someone further up the ridge. For a few minutes the noise was deafening, as bullets flew in both directions. One slug ripped through the brush and bounced off the rock just above my head. It buried itself in the dirt, three inches from my nose.

The rest of the day was less interesting. I heard men yell and shots, both near and far away from where

I hid. There were periods of silence that lasted nearly an hour. Several times I slept, only to be rudely awakened by noise. From listening to the men's speech, I gathered that I was in a Spanish speaking country.

Things got quiet toward evening. It was well after dark when I cautiously crawled out through the brush. I went back and checked both villas. Both were lit up like downtown on Saturday night. Crowds of people were congregated in the yards and on the patios. I could see the new leaders, or those who acted like bosses. At both places a man was standing on the back of a truck waving his arms and evidently making a speech. I shot both men and, just to confuse the situation further. To make them a little cautious I put a few rounds into each crowd without aiming at any one in particular. I didn't wait to see who, or how many others, I hit. I didn't care.

I retraced my path. I saw several patrols as I moved along. They were much more alert, and on guard, than when I first arrived. This made the going slow. It was nearly dawn when I approached the place where I had hidden the motor scooter. I was still a good fifty yards away when I heard, and saw, two men pulling the brush away from the scooter.

One of them took a two-way radio off his belt and held it up to his face. I saw his thumb press the talk bar just as my bullet caught him in the back of the neck. His companion sprang to his aid by instinct. Then his brain started working. He dove behind a tree and lay flat on the ground. I knew he was checking out his surroundings. He had not heard a shot, so he was not sure about where his adversary was positioned.

I knew he would have to raise his head in order to see me and I knew exactly where it was. His body was partially exposed and the crown of his hat was barely visible through the scope. About ten minutes passed before I saw that head lift. When his eyes were high enough so that he was looking directly at me I squeezed the trigger.

The motor scooter started on the first try. I was moving along the trail, for nearly an hour, before I remembered that I had not eaten in two days. There were field rations in the box under the scooter's seat, so I stopped for lunch. I was lucky. Under the trees, where I ate, the helicopter that went over hugging the treetops could not see me. If I had not stopped I might have been caught in the open.

I became much more alert. Since I had traveled the trail earlier, I was familiar with it, but it still took quite some time to find my destination. I was an hour early. Waiting, even this far from the chaotic scene I had left behind, was tedious. An hour seemed like a day, but when dusk came the plane landed.

When I got back to Japan I was "debriefed", which means I reported. That night I was free to prowl the many nightspots. The next morning I flew back to my unit in Korea with a group of six replacements for the base where I was stationed.

6.

A week later I was given orders, placing me on TDY to Okinawa. When I arrived at my new assignment my orders said I was to report to a Colonel B. Butler. I went directly to his office, and reported in. After this formality the Colonel opened a safe and handed me a large sealed envelope, with the comment, "Whatever it is that you are supposed to do is so secret that even I can't be told, and you are working for me. When you are ready, I have something that must be done, so don't forget who the boss is."

The Colonel sat behind his desk, and waited, while I opened the envelope. I could tell that he expected to be told something. My orders were on a small piece of "flash paper", of the kind magicians use. It had written on it, in pen, "Be at the Officer's Club tonight. You will be picked up by a girl in a bright blue dress. You will become, obviously to everyone, very friendly and leave with her. S.I.Y.T. Enjoy the book." The only other thing in the envelope was an innocent looking book. It was a novel about a female spy, who used her body as a weapon in the cold war. On the cover was the words, "Adult Entertainment".

After reading the note I touched my lighter to the paper. With a small puff of smoke my "orders" were gone. I looked at my temporary boss, laughed with him at the book's rating, and put it in my pocket. "Well sir, as soon as I get checked in at the BOQ (Bachelor Officer's Quarters), I'm going to clean up and put on a clean uniform. I plan to go over to the Officer's Club for the evening, then I think I'll read this book. I'll be too busy tomorrow, and the rest of my TDY for any celebrating." We exchanged salutes and I left.

I read the book. It told me all I needed to know about my assignment and contained a packet of powder that I would need to complete my job.

At eighteen hundred hours sharp I went to the Officer's Club. I had a steak dinner for the first time in a year and then moved to the far end of the bar. From that position I could observe the front door. I ordered a scotch-on-the-rocks and waited.

I could not help but wonder what she would look like, and if I could pick out the girl. Was she already there? Was she looking for me, even now? I knew she would know me. She would be looking for an Army Captain, and she knew the name. I wore a regulation uniform, and a regulation nameplate with a different name than my own. Besides, I was the only Army officer among all the Air Force types that occupied the room.

I didn't have any trouble recognizing the girl, and neither did anyone else. The entrance to the Officer's Club was slightly raised. It was as though there was a miniature stage two steps higher than the rest of the room. This, of course, was used as the grand entrance for formal affairs.

She came in, and stopped right on the edge of that little stage. There stood one on the most beautiful Oriental women I have ever seen. She stood about five feet seven inches, had raven black hair that shined like good lacquer. It hung down her back to her waist, without a hair out of place. Most of the Oriental women I have seen have had rather small breasts. Hers were large and looked even larger on her slim hourglass figure. She was wearing an off-the-shoulders, bright, blue gown with little black birds scattered about. It was so tight that it looked as though it was painted on.

The room had been rather noisy, with men talking to each other, or the occasional Oriental women in the club. A band was playing a slow dance tune and couples were on the dance floor. Suddenly all noise stopped. Someone in the band hit a sour note just as the music stopped. She stood there for a full minute, knowing that every eye was on her.

When she stepped off the entrance stage and started down those two steps there was an audible sigh, and then silence again. The dress was slit on both sides, all the way up to the sides of her hips. When she moved, she revealed first one, and then the other, long shapely leg, all of it.

She just kind of flowed across the room, smiling at her audience as she went. Every man there felt as though she was smiling only at him as she made eye contact with each one. She glided straight to my position in the back of the room. By the time she got to me I was standing. She said two words, "Let's dance".

I was glad I never had to say anything. I was still speechless. The noise of the club started up again and the band resumed playing. I guided her to the dance floor and took her into my arms. At first we danced much as one would dance with a sister. She started getting closer. Before long she was molded to me, as though we were one person. When the music stopped I wanted to keep going, but I led her to a secluded booth and ordered drinks.

We sat for over two hours, talking about everything and nothing. The longer we sat the friendlier we became. In the end, it was obvious to everyone that we were leaving to pursue our relationship in a more private setting. I actually felt the envy of all those Air Force officers as we headed, arm-in-arm, toward the door. The Colonel, to whom I had reported earlier in the day, was there with his wife. He nodded as I passed, without smiling, but I noticed the thumbs-up he gave me, out of sight of his wife.

Her car was brought up and she asked me to drive. I got in, while the lot boy held the passenger side door for her. It was while she was getting seated that I noticed that she was naked under her dress. She saw me staring, reached over and gently closed my mouth, and then gave me a kiss. It had both promise and passion all over it.

I put the car in gear and started toward my BOQ. The purpose of our meeting was temporarily forgotten. She brought me back to reality when she instructed me to make a right turn. For the first time her voice sounded like business. I followed instructions for twenty minutes, until she told me to park in front of a garage door at the end of a long building. She pressed the button on a controller and the door opened. We drove in. The door was completely closed before the interior lights turned on.

She started getting out of the car, giving me a big smile, and a free show as she moved. She said, "Follow me".

I thought, "You couldn't stop me".

She went through a door, with me right behind her. It was a large one room apartment, divided into areas. The center of the room was an open space. She walked directly to the center and turned to face me. I was about to speak when she raised her arms as though she expected me to dance with her. As she did this, a waltz started playing on the stereo in her living room area. I pulled her close and started dancing. About the time she molded her body to mine we were no longer dancing, just standing in one spot swaying back and forth ever so slightly.

She whispered, "Do you think we can find something to do until morning?"

I whispered back, "We'll work on it. I'm sure you can come up with an idea or two."

The rest of the night, and all of the next day she thought of things to do. If making love is an art form, she was Rembrandt. What started first as desire, became lust, and then became need. She completely took over my body, and my psyche. She could command her desired reaction in my body, and mind, simply by speaking a word or touching me. I realized that she was asking a number of strange questions, in the heat of passion, but I did not care.

It was nearly 3 a.m. when we made love for the final time. I knew I had told her everything she wanted to know in the time we spent together. I spotted at least one mike, in the base of the lamp on the night stand. I knew there had to be at least one more. I fixed more drinks, and lit cigarettes for both of us. Her cigarette was half gone when she fell asleep.

She was totally nude, sleeping peacefully on her back, and looking like a well-satisfied woman. Her drink spilled and the hand that held her smoke lay dangerously close to the alcohol. The fire didn't require much help getting started. It was smoldering when I got back into my uniform. I searched and found her tape recorder and a small box of tapes. As I went out the door fifteen minutes later I could see flames. It didn't bother her. She was dead within seconds after she fell asleep from the poison I had slipped into that last drink.

I was nearly two blocks away when I looked back and saw that the entire building was on fire. It would take a few minutes for anyone to discover the blaze at that early hour and a few more minutes for firefighters to arrive. All evidence of her involvement in espionage would be gone except, of course, for the six cassette tapes I had found when I searched her house. I had to have something to do while I waited for the flame to get a good start. They had different officer's names on them. With a five mile walk ahead of me, I wished I could have taken her car.

There were two things I was going to miss about that woman. One of them was that little sports car. The walk was not bad. I needed the exercise and the air, to clear my head. This assignment had been too close, and personal. The initials S.I.Y.T. that had appeared on my orders were there to inform me that she was my target. I found myself wishing she had been on our side.

I had gone nearly three miles, when two Air Police Corporals came along in a jeep. They informed me that I was wandering around in a pretty rough neighborhood and offered me a ride. They had the good sense not to question an officer about why he was there.

The officer my lady friend thought she was meeting was transferred to Japan. Arrangements were made for his wife to join him. He would not be tempted to stray again. Six other officers who had known the lady had their files tagged and were put in non-sensitive positions.

The TDY to Okinawa did not end with that one job. Colonel Butler had a problem in the Post Exchange. That was the reason for the original TDY request. The other thing was just a "side job". I spent a week auditing the books, and straightening out a mess. It was not so much a matter of theft, as was suspected. It was a matter of inept bookkeeping. While it was true that some petty thievery was going on, it was not as blatant as everyone seemed to think. I finished the job in five days and wrote my report. I turned it in to Colonel Butler on Monday.

7.

The very next day I was on an airplane to Japan. The city of Tokyo was not the modern, sophisticated city that it is today, at least the parts that I saw were not. It was a city of narrow streets, shacks, and mud. Trash was piled in vacant lots and rats ran about in broad daylight.

There was a person in Tokyo who was spying for the Russians. His arrest, and conviction, would have been a great embarrassment to the Japanese Government. He had to meet an untimely end. I was told that it would be better if his death could be blamed on a particular person in the Russian Embassy.

I was taken to a remote location, where the two men had a habit of meeting. They thought they were safe from prying eyes. I waited, in a dirty little hovel, nearby while some information, concerning a United States Government project was leaked. It seemed urgent enough for the two men to meet.

The Japanese showed up early, as usual. I walked up to him and asked for directions, making sure we were seen. I kept looking around as though being careful not to be spotted. After a minute I walked away quickly.

I knew the Russian would ask about me. KGB agents are, by nature, very suspicious minded. I knew he would mention something to his superiors. To sweeten the pot, I dropped a hint.

I got to flirting with a nice American girl, who was in the country as part of a Red Cross project. Just to be friendly, I took her to lunch. The place we chose for our meal happened to be the same one that the KGB type and some other members of the Russian Embassy often went for their lunch. By chance we sat quite close to one of their tables.

During our conversation the girl asked me if I was stationed in Japan. I informed her that I was not in the service. I'll never forget her next question. It was as though it was rehearsed, and planned. "Well then, what are you doing in Tokyo?" She emphasized the "are".

I looked her square in the eye for a moment. Then I whispered, just loud enough so I could be overheard, "I work for the CIA. I met a man last night who is going to help us nab a Russian spy."

After that, she got friendlier, and we talked about more personal things. She hinted that she would like to see what the nightlife in Tokyo was like, but I ignored the invitation. I thought it was too bad I didn't have time to teach her a few of the things I had learned from that Chinese girl on Okinawa. Those thoughts, and my visualization of this blonde beauty, in that shining blue dress with the little birds on it, made me decide to end our luncheon date before I forgot my job.

It was not until later that afternoon that I "happened" to meet my target on the street. I walked up to him, shook his hand, and said, "I want to thank you for your help last evening. I got exactly what I wanted. You were a great help". The man looked confused, but he was gracious and smiled. Oriental men have such good manners. I was sure that, by now, he was under surveillance.

That same night the two men met at their usual rendezvous. I could see through my night vision binoculars that they were arguing. I decided to let the "pot" boil. For the next two days I was "seen" around the target. Once, coming out of a building at the same time. He even greeted me a couple times.

Information, that the KGB agent would know was phony, was "inadvertently" given to the Japanese traitor. He called for a meeting. Another date, this time with a redhead, for luncheon at the cafe let the Russians know he might be walking into a trap. During the conversation I told the redhead that I would be going back to Washington. When she asked why, I told her that my business there would be done in "a day or two".

That was all it took. The argument, at the remote meeting place, was even more violent than the first. Through the long lens I was using, I could see my target sweating. He reached toward his back pocket, probably to get a handkerchief, of maybe a gun.

The Russian got off the first shot, but both men got hit several times. Neither man was much of a shot, even at such close range. The Japanese lay dead. Two men, I recognized as Embassy Staff, rushed up. They made sure the traitor was dead, by shooting him in the head. Then they carried their man away, badly wounded.

Early the next morning the Russian Embassy issued a statement that the Russian had taken ill quite suddenly. The press release said he had been flown to Moscow for treatment. By noon, the Newspapers, Police, Russian Embassy, and the Japanese Government all received an envelope by special delivery. The envelope contained infrared pictures that clearly showed the Diplomat shooting the Japanese traitor, and the two Embassy employees helping the killer.

There was no indication that the Japanese man was a traitor. Both the news media, and the police thought it was an out-and-out murder. When the story hit the headlines the Russian Embassy was forced to admit that there had been something going on, but did not admit to any treasonous acts. Their official statement claimed that it was an altercation over a woman.

My job was done. It was the first time I never personally put someone down. I had been seen too often to suit me. I decided to have it checked out. In investigating the murder, the police found not one witness that remembered anything that could remotely connect me to the incident. Sources the CIA had developed said that there those who remembered the two instances in the cafe. They remembered the conversation. They could describe the girls, but not the man that was sitting with them. Not being one to borrow trouble, I flew back to Okinawa. Both girls suddenly received promotions, and were transferred back to the United States.

Back on Okinawa, orders were waiting for me. I was to return to Korea, clear my desk and process out, for my return to the continental United States. My tour of duty in Korea was over. I wondered about my "other assignment" would it also terminate. It did not!

8.

When I went to Korea I spent eighteen days on the water with nearly three thousand other men. When I returned to "Stateside", I flew, with six other officers. Once we landed, I was separated from the others and put on a leer jet, bound for Washington D.C.

It was dark when we landed and I was transported in a limousine with darkened windows. At the destination I walked into a plush apartment. Jim was waiting for me. He said I had eighteen hours to sleep and relax in the apartment. He asked if there was any thing I needed. I said, "A big steak about two inches thick, and a blonde - in that order".

He said, "I'll see that you get the steak". He picked up the telephone and placed the order. As he headed for the door, he said, "I'll see you in eighteen hours, we'll talk then."

A few minutes later the meal was delivered. The server was a cute Auburn haired girl who was very outgoing and friendly. I asked her to join me. We finished eating and relaxed. We were lying on the couch, watching television. I was telling her that I had not been in a bed for three days.

All of a sudden it was ten hours later. The television was playing kid's cartoons and I had a girl curled up beside me, sound asleep. Carefully, I got off the couch and went into the bedroom to "peel" off the uniform I had been wearing since I left Korea. I was enjoying a hot shower when she joined me. Three hours later she left, with last night's dirty dishes. She returned with steak and eggs breakfast for two. We were just finishing the meal when the telephone rang and she had to leave.

Jim arrived exactly on time. We talked about half an hour before he dropped his new assignment on me. I knew the plush treatment was for a purpose. "You are going to Germany tonight. There is an Englishman there who needs to be sent to his reward. Don't ask me why. I don't know the answer."

I was not enthusiastic about the job. "The Army owes me better than a month of leave time and I was hopping to take a vacation. Germany was not my first choice. If I do this one I will not be fully alert. I could louse it up and that would cause the government a problem. It would not bother me, personally, because I'd be dead."

Jim apologized, "I know we have been using you a lot. Four of the people who trained with you are dead. There are only two of you left. We have recruited others, but they are not experienced, and not as good. We've had two people doing the work of seven".

"Give me the details", I said, with a sigh, "but after this job I want to relax for at least a month."

Jim agreed. He said there was nothing more on the "drawing board", so there would be no big problem.

Sometimes a person can do no wrong and luck rides his shoulders. My trip to Germany was quick. The jet I was on landed and I went directly to where my information said the Englishman would be at that time of night. I arrived as he was leaving a nightclub in the sleazy part of town. He had not gone a block when I stepped out of the shadows and hit him over the head with a two-by-four I'd stumbled over. I dragged him into an alley, ransacked his pockets, took his money, and slit his throat with his own knife.

The jet, on which I arrived, had just finished refueling when I boarded it for my return flight. The Englishman's watch, ring, money, and knife were dropped into the Atlantic Ocean. I was back in the apartment, in Washington D.C., eating another steak, twenty-four hours after I had left. The same red headed girl was my server. My friend could not figure out why I was so tired. She thought I had been in the apartment, sleeping, the whole time.

Jim could not believe it. He would not accept my story until he got a report from Germany. It said the Englishman had been robbed, and murdered, by a mugger.

I was invited to meet the Commander In Chief and taken to the Oval Office. He thanked me for my service and gave me a medal.

The Army ordered me to a post in New Mexico and assigned me the job of Documents Officer. I had forty-five days to report, thirty days leave and fifteen days travel time. I spent the time in the mountains of Idaho. I rented a cabin, in the woods, and went fishing. I did not relish the idea of cooking, cleaning, and doing chores, so I took the redhead along. She was a great cook, but we had to hire a local woman to clean and do chores; we were too busy.

9.

As a general rule, the intelligence reports I received were very accurate. There were times that unforeseen circumstances made anything I knew about a subject utterly useless. There was one, particularly difficult job, where good information was vital.

This particular job was inside the United States, so there could be no questions about the circumstances of the individual's demise. There had been six tries taken at this target and all of them failed miserably. The closest anyone had come was to make him sick to his stomach after eating poisoned food.

I was to make another attempt. The orders were to make it look natural, or accidental, if possible. If not, eliminate him at all cost. That meant, even if it cost my own life. I studied him for a week. I studied the documents I had received, and the man himself. I knew his habits, and his routine. It was going to be difficult.

I got access to his automobile and fixed a wheel in such a way that, when he turned left, and applied his breaks, the left front wheel would lock in place. I had a particular spot in mind. When the man got to the place everything worked perfectly, except that he was driving too slowly. He crumpled a fender.

The locked wheel pulled the car around. The right front fender hit a guardrail post. The car continued to spin around, until his right rear fender also hit the railing. That is where the car stopped. If he had been going five miles per hour faster it would have rolled down an embankment. The man was hardly even shaken when he got out of the vehicle, to inspect the damage. I could have put him away right there, but I still had hopes of an accident.

The only good chance, for an assassination, appeared to be as he entered his office building. It was the only consistent thing about his daily routine. He entered the building precisely at eight thirty every weekday morning. Over a hundred yards to the east was a vacant building. It was condemned and would become the victim of a wrecking ball, within a few days.

The deadline was near, so I decided to do the shot. It would be entirely possible to get out of the building, and away, before anyone could spot me. Just as always, precisely at eight thirty, he emerged from his vehicle and started up the steps toward the front door. He always went directly into the building, so I was prepared to drop him as he pulled the door open.

This particular morning, a panhandler came along. My target stopped to talk, and give the man some money. "So much the better", I thought. "This will give me time for a better shot". The scope I was using allowed me to "zero in". With most scopes I would see the head, and part of the torso. With the telephoto feature, I could narrow the field down to see an area two inches in diameter. The crosshairs only pinpointed the location of entry. If I could see the target through the lenses, he was dead. I had everything lined up, and started zeroing in on the temple area, when the target disappeared.

Looking over the scope, I could see my man crumpled on the steps. I quickly widened my field of vision and took a careful look, using the scope as a telescope. The panhandler was frozen in place. His mouth was opening, and closing, as though he was screaming at the full capacity of his lungs, but no sound came out. As I watched, he got control of his voice and yelled for help. Several people came rushing over, including a police officer. The officer called the paramedics. Someone started CPR., Others just stood and watched.

I put the rifle away. It broke down so that it fit in an attaché case. I arrived at the scene, wearing a business suit and carrying the attaché case. I stopped to watch as the Fire Department Paramedics did their job. I was close enough to catch any word about the man's condition. It was only a couple minutes later that I heard one of the Medics say, "Looks like a massive coronary. This guy was dead before he hit the ground".

I had stalked that man for over two weeks. I knew all there was to know about him. He had gotten away from several assassins', mostly because of luck. Just as I was about to "drop a hammer on him", he got away again. I was relieved. This time he got away permanently.

I never did convince Jim, that I had nothing to do with what happened. I was talking to him about that job when I was bothered by a fly. I quickly caught the bug and slapped it against my leg. A while later I did the same thing with another fly. That was when Jim started calling me "flyswatter". Our business was "swatting flies" and I was his prime "flyswatter", or so he said.

We had acquired a new Commander In Chief and he wanted to meet me. I couldn't convince him that I had done nothing to get rid of the problem either. He awarded me another Medal.

It was after that job that I began to be told why they wanted someone gone. Until then I had no idea, and never asked. After that job I seemed to have gained a "reputation" of sorts. I started getting the more difficult assignments, generally after other attempts had been botched.

10.

I was given two assignments at the same time. I was to eliminate one and then immediately move to the other. It was an example of poor Intel. Or else it was coincidence. One was a drug dealer and powerful politician in one country and the other was the same but in another country. They happened to be related.

I came into the country on a private airplane as a tourist. My weapon was there waiting for me so I hand no problem with customs. I looked the part right down to the camera. I checked into a hotel and went looking for a spot to get my man when he arrived at a local restaurant. He was known to have dinner there at the same time every day. It was always late in the evening. My shot would have to be made after dark with no more light than that which the street and commercial lights gave. With a night scope my only concern was the flash of the muzzle. The silencer would take care of most and just maybe all of it.

I found the right spot on the roof of a building some hundred yards away. It was a business that would be closed by the time I needed it and there was a way to gain the roof without much trouble. It was only three stories and had a fire escape in back. There was a ladder that went from the top of the fire escape to the roof. Of course I would have to find a way to pull the bottom steps down since they were up in the air. In case of a fire, a person's weight would lower the final steps from the second story. I got a rope and tied a weight on the end to lasso those steps. That night I pulled the steps down and climbed onto the roof half an hour before my target would appear.

I got ready for his arrival and waited. I watched through a rectangular hole built into the roof for water drainage so no one would see me up there. I was hoping to use it for my shot as well. At one time there was a metal deflector to direct the water form the roof downward but it had long since rusted off.

My target's limo stopped and not one but two men were getting out. I had studied the photos of both of my targets and recognized both men. Their bodyguards were alert and watched the area closely. One guard went into the restaurant ahead of the two men. The other followed a little way behind. I had my sights on them and waited for my opportunity.

The front bodyguard held the door open for the two to enter. My targets were entering one behind the other when I squeezed the trigger. The slug went through the back one ripping a hole in his heart. It hit something inside that deflected it up slightly on its way through. It hit the man in front in the neck and cut open the carotid artery. Once leaving that man it was through and lodged in a wall. The one died instantly and the other bleed out before anyone could help him. I had gotten two men with one shot.

There was a lot of commotion down there. The bodyguards were looking around with their guns out. People ran in all directions. It was a good thing I had shot through that rectangle hole. I broke the weapon apart and push the barrel down a sewer vent pipe. The stock went into a ventilator shaft. I had no gun or ammunition. That done I scrambled down the ladder and fire escape.

When I came out of the alley I was stopped and searched by a policeman. He asked what I was doing behind the building so I told him I was just relieving my bladder. He let me go on my way. I became a tourist for a couple of days and then left.

Jim was pleased that I had finished the job so quickly and surprised that I had gotten two with one shot. I'm not sure he believed me when I told him the second man was an accident. I meant to put both men down but I thought I would need to take a second shot to do it. I knew I would wound him, but to kill him? No.

11.

As I said, intelligence reports are valuable. When the target has had several attempts on his life, he becomes careful. Most of them have bodyguards. It is not always feasible to try getting the man alone. This one was so paranoid that his guards never left him, even while he was sleeping.

Information obtained told us that this man would make a trip once a month, to visit his mother. He always stayed at one particular motel the first night, then continued on the next morning. By nightfall he would be back at the motel. Early in the day, one of his employees would rent three cabins, for two nights, but not always the same three cabins. The guards would occupy the cabins on either side, while the man would take the middle one.

At least one guard stayed with the subject at all times. When the man left the motel for his day with his mother, guards would stay in his cabin. They must have been well paid, they never slacked off from their duties. Only the maid was allowed into the cabin. She was closely watched. Always, he insisted on the same maid, and he tipped her generously, to assure her loyalty.

Therefore she did extra things for him. One of those things was to leave him a small container of baby powder, that she carried on her cart whenever she knew he would be there. He liked to powder his feet, before putting on his socks.

There were rooms to clean before she arrived at the target's quarters. By ten, she was ready to enter the room of her favorite guest, who always treated her so very well, because he would arrive soon. With meticulous care, she cleaned the room and made the bed, under the watchful eyes of the guards.

The last thing she did was to go out to her cleaning cart, pick up her sampler-sized container of baby powder and place it on the counter of the bathroom. It rested in the center of a lace doily. She always used a new one that had never had the seal broken. One of the guards handed her an envelope, which contained her tip, patted her bottom, and sent her on her way.

The target was late getting in that night. There had been some trouble in town that had delayed his departure. No sooner than he entered his room, he went to bed. Early the next morning one of his men woke him. He showered and then began to dress. He smiled to himself as he picked up the baby powder, broke the seal, and generously powdered his feet. Afterward, he sprinkled his shoulders and chest with the fine powder, emptying the container, and tossed it in the wastebasket. He probably thought to himself that he would give the maid a bonus, for her continued thoughtfulness.

He chose to wear a bright red silk shirt, dark blue slacks, dark blue socks, and a pair of very expensive custom made shoes. Two of his guards remained at the motel, while two more accompanied their boss. The man did not eat breakfast, which would be waiting for him. One bodyguard acted as chauffeur, while the other rode "shotgun" beside him in the front of the big Cadillac limousine.

Twenty-two miles from the motel, they turned up a gravel road. Two miles up the gravel road, they turned up a narrow lane, the "shotgun" rider got out of the car. It was his job to see that no other vehicle went up that road. A mile and a half up the lane the Limo stopped in front of a well-kept lodge.

Two men, dressed as though they were lumberjacks, came out to greet the visitor, and welcome him. These were the men who kept the grounds, tended the animals and were responsible for security. Both of them were wanted for murder in several places.

Two women were waiting on the porch. One was his mother. The other was there as a companion to his mother. Actually, she was a registered nurse who had shot her husband after a quarrel. She had slept with the target a few times and needed a place to hide. He put her there because of her medical background, and her ability to cook, not because he felt anything for her.

The subject's mother was not in the best of health. She had had a stroke, and lost most of the use of her left arm. She greeted her son with obvious pride. She was very proud of his success, although she was not sure what he did. All she knew was that he rode in a limousine with a chauffer, wore the best clothing, and always had plenty of money. He doted on her, supporting her lavishly. Anything she wanted, he provided.

Once each month, she could count on him to leave his busy life in the city and visit her. On the monthly visit he always paid the workers and left money for her. She knew her son had built the lodge for his own use, but whenever she visited, she always said she would like to live there. When she had her "sickness", he moved her to the lodge to recuperate. She had been living there four years.

The man gave his mother a big hug, ate a hearty breakfast, paid the "help", and settled down for a relaxing visit. It was a warm day and his feet began to perspire, as they sat on the porch. He was grateful for the powder that his favorite maid had left for him. In the afternoon, he went out to his car and brought in an attaché case.

He went up to his private study and sat the attaché beside seven others. Each one was full of money. He locked the door to the room and went down to eat the evening meal. He said his farewells and left. He didn't even know when his driver picked up the other guard, he was very tired and slept during the drive back to his motel cabin.

Back in the room, he sat down to watch television for a little while. The next thing he knew, it was morning. He got out of his clothes, showered, and dressed in an expensive suit. He had used all of his baby powder, so he didn't dust his tired feet. He threw the dirty socks into a wastebasket and wore new ones. He never liked dirty socks in his overnight bag. He thought they made everything smell.

They left the motel shortly after ten in the morning, a little later than usual. About five miles along the road he drifted off to sleep again. His guards kept quiet, so as not to disturb him. That evening, when they arrived at his house in the city, the guards discovered that he was dead.

I knew why the man was so paranoid about security. There had been several attempts on his life. I was never told what he did to make his money, but it had to be crooked. The only thing I knew, for sure, was that he was my assignment. It was not possible to get to him in the city, so the only thing to do was to kill him while on the trip he made, on the same day, every month.

I knew his car had bulletproofing. That had been tried. His men had always been successful in screening him when he was not in his house, office, or car. Three of them had been killed during previous attempts. It was going to have to be subtle, and sneaky.

While researching the possibilities, I rented a cabin at the same motel where he always stayed. The motel had individual cabins that were scattered in groups of three across a three, or four, acre field. Reservations had been made for cabins seven, eight, and nine. My man would be arriving in two weeks. I gleaned that information from the maid.

I met the maid "accidentally", at a local tavern that she frequented. She was slightly over forty and somewhat heavy, so she was quite flattered when a young man began buying her drinks. As we talked, she told me about her rich customer, and his use of the baby powder. I was "quite taken" with the idea of sprinkling ones feet, so I talked her into letting me have one of the samplers for my own use.

The next day I sent the powder to my boss, with a note explaining what I wanted. Two days later the container was delivered to me at a hotel room in the city. I checked into cabin number one at the motel two days before the subject was due to arrive.

My expressed purpose, for returning, was to visit with my friend, the maid. We spent our nights together and each morning I would help her get her maid's cart organized. On the third day I told her I would have to leave right after I got her started on her rounds. "My vacation was over". While helping her with the cart, I made sure she had only one baby powder sampler - mine.

162

As the target's feet began to sweat, the poison in the powder began to be absorbed into his blood stream. Within a few hours it began to work on his system. By using the powder on his upper torso, and leaving his socks on during the night, he hastened his demise.

The socks, and baby powder container, that he left behind, were burned. The maid came to clean and emptied the trash into the incinerator. Burning trash was the policy of the motel, to help eliminate much of the bulk and save expenses. Even if there had been an investigation, there was no trace of how the poison was administered. The newspaper account of his death listed natural causes. Just so there would be no questions, I went back to visit my "girl friend" one more time, a month later.

We were sitting up against the headboard of the bed, having a cigarette, and a drink, when she told me about her new job. Her rich friend had died suddenly and all of the help at his mother's house had left. His mother had found several million dollars hidden in her son's room, so she didn't have any money worries. The maid told me she, and her husband, were going to be her new "crew". She had never mentioned a husband once, during the six, or eight times we has been together. I thought it interesting that she never mentioned him during, what would be, our last rendezvous, until "after".

12.

It was after I returned to duty that I learned about politics and the military. I was back in the States less than four months when I was "RIFED". That is, I was caught in a "Reduction in Force". The Army decided they had too many officers, so they reduced a lot of us to our permanent enlisted grade. I went from captain to corporal over night. I went from Documents Officer, to Documents Clerk. I was working for a Warrant Officer who used to work for me. I liked that Warrant, and I stayed out of his way. I was on "TDY" most of the time anyway.

The first "TDY" was a "quickie". I was picked up at Kirkland field and flown into South America. I read the file on my target while on the airplane, so it was easy to find him. An hour later he died of lead poisoning. He was driving down the road from his home, when someone shot him through the head. The car ran off the road, into a ditch and rolled over. I was back at my desk the next morning.

A month after I became an enlisted man, I was given a chance to get back my bars. I was called to the Base Commander's office. I wondered what was going on. When I was demoted, I had checked with Jim. He said there was little he could do, to intercede on my behalf would give someone the idea I had some connections I was not supposed to have. Now I had been summoned.

At the Commanding General's office I was ushered into a closed room, just off the "War Room". At the time I was the only enlisted man with access clearance for that room. It was where the Army's most secret documents were held, and where top-secret meetings were conducted. I was warmly greeted by a full Colonel, from Military Intelligence.

He started by asking me how I would like to have my commission returned, permanently. That got my attention. The Colonel sweetened the pot. He said I would be a Major within two months after I did a "little chore" for him. I had been across a street, or two, and even made it all the way around a block one time. I asked what "little chore"?

They say that every man has a double. I began to believe it. He showed me a picture and asked me to identify the man it portrayed. It was I, and I told him as much. He disagreed. "It only looks like you Captain." We want you to take this man's place for a while.

The man had been stationed near Pusan, Korea. Just before he was to return to the United States, he died under mysterious circumstances. This enlisted man had a Top-Secret Restricted Data security clearance and had been working with very sensitive documents.

The investigating officer was one I had known, casually, while I was stationed in Korea. He thought I was the one that had been killed. Military Intelligence had to know if something had been compromised.

A bazaar scheme began to roll into being. They would substitute me, for him, until they could clear up the matter of his death, and learn what, if anything, he had been disclosed.

I was the only person that could easily fill that role. I would be working for Military Intelligence. The Colonel gave me two days to think it over. It didn't take two days. I was young and eager. I was promised my commission back, a promotion, and even a substantial "reenlistment" bonus. I believed every word the Colonel said. I would have done it anyway, because my government asked for my help.

Once I told the Colonel that I would do his "little chore", he dropped his bomb. The man was married and had children, but he and his wife had had some conflicts. He had been gone over a year, so he figured she would consider the differences between us were caused by the separation. People change in Korea.

The only problem with the switching of identities, was the body. There was a dead man. There had to be an accounting for that body. After altering paperwork and military records, I was officially dead. I was, now, another person.

Before I volunteered for the job, I checked with my contact, Jim. He thought the prospects were interesting. He told me that things were quieted down in his department. He said "If anyone can pull this off for the Army, you are the man."

I gave my agreement, with not a little reluctance. I would be another man, for a while. I was flown by helicopter out to the troop ship the man was supposed to be riding. He was a quiet, Bible reading, individual who never mixed with the other men. I just listened to their conversations with a deadpan expression, and read the Bible. When I was alone I read up on "myself".

He wanted to go to a Bible College and become a minister. Reading the Bible was part of his life. There was one close call aboard the ship. Out on deck, I met a man whom I had seen a couple times before I left Korea. He started to speak, then stopped and looked at my uniform. "You know Corporal, I know a Captain that looks exactly like you."

I looked him square in the eye and replied, "Maybe I have a twin and don't know it."

The man began to get more and more into the comparison. I turned the conversation around to religion. He suddenly decided he was late reporting for a detail. I hoped I would not see him again. I almost ran into him twice more, but each time he avoided me. He didn't want me preaching to him again.

My "wife" was not waiting at the dock with the other wives. It was not until we were through processing in that she contacted me through personnel. When we finally got together she was so cold toward me, her "husband", that I honestly thought my cover was blown. I soon discovered that she didn't much like her husband, but she was not about to set him free. His particular religious beliefs did not favor divorce, and he wanted to be a preacher. I went along with the program.

The kids were staying with her parents and I didn't get to meet them until I had been discharged from the Processing Center, and assigned a new post, with some leave time.

We traveled to visit her folks, and get the kids. I helped on the farm for a few days. It almost caused a problem. Her Dad began to wonder about me. He mentioned, not a few times, "I didn't know you knew how to do that". All I was doing was normal farm work.

I would look at him and say, "There are a lot of things you don't know about me."

I think the man actually started to like me. The new post was in Oklahoma. I was to be a clerk in the supply room of a training outfit. It was an easy job. I took my "family" to a local church and settled in to my new life as supply clerk and apprentice preacher. I soon became the associate pastor with responsibility for the youth and the choir.

Once a month I was to report, in writing, on my progress. The first month's report brought me sharp criticism. All I did was to mention that I thought the man died of fright. After being away from the witch he married for so long, the thought of returning to her probably scared him to death.

The bedroom had been one of our concerns. There was no need to worry. She wanted nothing what-so-ever to do with that part of marriage. We tolerated each other "for the sake of the kids". The one thing she had noticed that was different about me was that I would not take any of her "guff". She would start an argument, and I would tell her to shut her "yap", then I would walk out. That really made her mad.

Eventually I was mustered out and started school. Being a person who likes history, and loved school, I took to the college like a duck to water. Although the Army was still paying me I still had to work, in order to keep my cover, and support the family. My military pay was sent to me as GI Bill payments. Working eight hours, going to school six hours, spending time studying, and catching some sleep whenever I could did two things for me. I got a great education in the history of the Christian religion as well as the Jewish religion. It, also, kept me away from the witch.

If I kept to the agenda I would graduate in two years, with a three year THG (General Theology) Degree. I soon discovered that the degree was not "accredited", but I found a college that would accept the credits, and give me an accredited degree. A transfer of credits from the Bible College, and one of the regular colleges I had attended were all I needed. To get the degree I would have to take at least one course from the institution. Of course there was the minor problem of my name. I figured Jim would have a solution for that.

My assignment actually ended while I was still in the Bible College. I was supposed to be attending a ministerial conference, but I made a detour. I made my final report before a board of six officers, a General, three full Colonels and two Lieutenant Colonels. Not one of them had been involved in soliciting me for the job. When I finished speaking, and handed in my report, I was congratulated for a job well done. When the General mentioned that he was going to have me promoted to Sergeant, things got a little tedious.

I said, "I'm sorry sir, but that would be quite a demotion, since I am a Captain, not a Corporal."

He looked down at a folder marked "Top-Secret". It contained my service records. "It says here that you were reduced to your permanent grade, which is Corporal. There is nothing in this record about being reinstated."

I tried to explain the deal I had made, and even told him the name of the authorizing officer.

He told me that the deal could not have been made, because it was illegal and against government policy. It was then that the conversation began to get hot.

Two Lieutenant Colonels, three full Bird Colonels, and a General were all chewing me out at the same time. I was chewing back, just as vigorously. The whole argument ended abruptly when the General stood up and said, "You'll do as you are damn well ordered to do soldier!"

That got to me. With a few expletives, I let him know what he could do with his orders. I ended my suggestions with, "You had better take another look at my enlistment papers, I out-rank you mister, and I don't have to do a damn thing you say, or follow anyone's orders, my enlistment was up six months ago, I'm a civilian." With that I walked out. When I sneaked a look the General was looking at my records with his mouth open. I read his lips, "Well I'll be dammed".

That afternoon I contacted Jim. I was ready to tell him what he, and the government, could do with my "other" job as well. Jim sounded as though he expected my call. All he said was, "I have been waiting for you. I'll be landing in three hours. Go have a couple drinks and relax. I think you know I am acquainted with your favorite watering hole."

As I waited, I could not help but think, "Jim must have majored in psychology. This is just what I needed." That was after my third scotch-on-the-rocks. By then I was feeling little pain. I've never been a heavy drinker anyway, and after being a tee-totaler for a period of time, it hit me hard.

I realized that I could be in a lot of trouble. When I took a Commission, I agreed to be on active duty or in the reserves, more or less at the military's discretion, not mine, until I was sixty-five. The General, and his subordinates, were most likely to think more than twice.

If word got out about the fraud the Army had perpetrated the publicity would cause a lot of people their jobs. The government would have to pay millions to one widow, and her three sons. The newspapers, and a Congressional Committee would have a field day.

I knew that at that very moment I could be a target. My sudden demise would save a lot of embarrassment. One of the traits the government sought in their "special profile" people was that they could not hold life in high esteem. In truth, I was just that way.

Death held no mystery for me. I had seen too many people die, to be afraid of it. One thing I had learned: when a man is dead, you can't hurt him. That, in itself, could make death almost preferable to life.

These morbid thoughts were interrupted by a familiar voice. "Well, old man, I see you took my advice. You look about as relaxed and laid back as I've ever seen you. You ready to get serious?"

I motioned him to a chair, "I guess I got a little out of control, but I know I was right. How did you get the word so quickly?" He suggested that we move to a small meeting room in the back of the establishment. It would be quieter, and there would be no chance of someone listening.

Nothing Jim did surprised me anymore. "Remember that Bird Colonel that was fairly quiet? He had secret orders to report every thing that went on in that room. He thought he was reporting to the Pentagon, but he was talking to me. I can tell you this, if you want me to do it, I can get your commission back and put this whole incident behind you. You know I can blackmail with the best of them.

"The only problem we have is that our influence is extremely delicate. We don't actually exist, officially. Any President, in the future, could eliminate us without realizing it. The end of the cold war, a victory over drugs, or half dozen other unforeseeable things could affect our agency. I, for one, would like to see us become obsolete, but I'll serve as long as I'm needed, or unable to perform satisfactorily."

It became my turn to philosophize, "Do you have any idea how complicated this is? I would do it again, because my government asked, but right now we have a big mess. I'll never volunteer to do anything like that for Army Intelligence again.

"At the least we have a mess to clean up. I've been thinking the situation over for three or four hours. I think I have come up with the most risk free, logical, solution. Right now I need some food in my stomach. I haven't eaten because I've been waiting for you to pay the bill. As of right now I'm unemployed."

Jim wanted something. He agreed to pay for our dinners, and drinks, just a little too quickly. It is disconcerting to have someone know you better than you know yourself. He ordered the meal exactly as I wanted, before I even looked at a menu. It is very difficult to deal with someone who knows what you have on you mind, and what "buttons" to push to get his own way. I knew "going in" that I was beat. My only hope was that he would let me think everything was my idea.

We ate in silence. Over coffee I told him my plan. "Jim, we killed me off a while back. I am now condemned to live with the most horrendous woman you have ever met and committed to the ministry. If we correct that mess we are in big trouble. If we leave the situation alone I am condemned to a living hell. There is a tremendous risk that I will be discovered to be a fraud. If that happens, we're in a bigger mess. If I take back my commission I have to do it under my true name, so we're in hot water again. I have a way out. As far as I can see it is the only solution."

Jim nodded his head, "Flyswatter, we have known each other for quite a while now. The nature of our business is such that there is no such thing as a friend. You are as close to me as anyone. Whatever you have on your mind, I'll listen. We will work this whole thing out here and now. Then we'll do it. You can dictate terms to your heart's content and get everything you want out of the Army."

I leaned back with a cup of coffee in my hand. I let the silence bear down as I drank about half the cup while formulating my thoughts. "Jim, you are about as full of it as a Thanksgiving turkey. Calling me Flyswatter, or even a friend, would not stop either of us from putting the other down permanently without blinking an eye. You know I would never blackmail the government. It is not my style. Now that we've cleared away the bull, here's what I have in mind.

"The witch will never know, because she doesn't care. I like the courses I'm taking and I want to graduate. You know how I am about school. I don't have a lot to do with that woman that thinks she married me, but I love the kids. She works, and runs around on me. I work, go to school, study, and watch the boys. I'll just continue the status-quo for a while. When the time is right, or I can't stand it anymore, I 'kill' myself. Then I'll resume my identity.

"My file is classified Top-Secret. Get it upgraded to Q. That safeguard may be valuable. As for the rest, I'm mad at the government, but I'm still an American. You can get mad at your parents, but they remain your parents. I'll get over it."

Jim was not one to show emotion. When I saw the little smirk at the corner of his mouth I knew I had played right into his agenda. The first words out of his mouth confirmed the fact. He read my eyes as he spoke. "I can see it is not `snow-job' time. You just said exactly what I wanted to hear, not in detail, but close to it. I apologize. I really thought I would have to con you. You're right about another thing. I would put you down, if ordered. We are in the `fly swatting' business, but I wouldn't like it.

"While we are being honest I'll tell you something else. This department we fondly call `the

173

company', or 'the office', did not originate when you were recruited. It started during the Second World War. I've been around a lot of years longer than you. All I am is a glorified dispatcher, or maybe a coordinator. I spent my time in the field, but that was a while back. There are a great number of people who work for the Department, but none of them know about our particular office.

"There are only six of us and we're so secret that 'we do not exist'. Only two people know more than two others that work for the office. Our orders come from one man, and one man only. That man is the Commander In Chief. When the office wants someone to swat a fly, you can darn well bet the fly needs swatting.

"The Department is large, powerful, and well known. It doesn't get the publicity that the CIA and the FBI get. It's low profile. We have access to data banks you would never believe. The 'office' only works like the tip of a spear. We do the dirty work.

"At this time you are the sole survivor of your group. You have lasted longer, without getting discovered, than anyone in the history of our operation. Only two people have ever survived more than four years. I'm one, you're the other. Two of our best were eliminated trying to get that one you got on the steps to his office. I still don't know how you induced a fatal heart attack, and I'm not sure I want to know.

"You have lasted longer, in the field, than anyone. I know it's bucking the odds, but we're going to need you. I need you to teach those we recruit and train. You are the best we've ever had. We need that expertise if others are to be effective and survive. From now on you will be completely informed as to why the subject should be gone. You will now know why the fly needs swatted. You will get a substantial bonus for every job you complete."

After that long-winded, sugar coated, speech, I knew two things. I now had some input, and would be better informed, and that he had more work. I thought for a full minute, before I made a decision that has proved to be not in my own best interests financially, or in the area of job security, or even in the area of a future. At the time I did not expect to live all that long anyway. Like he said, I was bucking the odds.

"Jim, I will do as you wish, I think you already know that. I'll teach, or write a lesson plan. I'll kill for the government, but I can't take pay for it in the form of a bonus. If I did I would only be a hired hit man. I see little difference, then, between a criminal and me. Leave my records classified 'Q', but have the company hold them. It would be better if I remain dead, just in case I got sloppy back there someplace."

"OK" he replied, "Now I have to drop another piece of information on you. Because of the nature of your work in the Army, and the information you handled, the FBI has been asked by the military to keep tabs on you. The head of the FBI has turned that job over to the Department. That's normal procedure. The Department gathers information for the CIA, BIA, ATF, DEA, FBI, the Secret Service, the rest of the alphabet, and even all branches of the military. The Department gathers information for everyone. For the rest of your life you will be monitored. This may make our communications more difficult. You'll have to be careful what you say on the telephone. It may be our own Department, but what we do is not for just anyone to know. This is for your own protection, as well as for national security.

"By the way, you have been officially assigned to Military Intelligence with the rank of Major. The reason for this is that MI is better at keeping records secret and no one will get your records for any reason. Your records have the highest possible classification and they do not show what assignments you have had, only that you were loaned out another agency form time to time. They still say you audited books. They say you were honorably discharged back before you took on that assignment for MI. You are on inactive reserve. You will be working for about every agency in government from time to time but you will always have military rank and privileges when you work. The problem is you are not officially in the military so you have been and will be "recalled" whenever you are needed.

I had to leave. "Well let's leave everything as we agreed. Right now I have to get on the road. I'm supposed to be at a preacher's meeting and I said I would be back by now. I'll be about five hours late. The witch gets all bent out of shape when I'm late. If you need me you can figure out a way to contact me. You call me, I won't call you.

13.

A month later I got recalled for another assignment. As a cover, I got an invitation to a "Fellowship Meeting". The only way I could arrange to go alone was to ask my "wife" to accompany me. As long as she thought I wanted her along, she would refuse to go. She said she could not take off from work. What she meant was, "Wow an opportunity to spend more time with my boss." She was not thinking of work.

Once away from the house I drove to an airport a hundred miles to the west. An hour later I was on a jet headed for El Paso, Texas. I was briefed in my hotel room.

There was a Police Captain from the Northwest, who took a vacation twice a year in old Mexico. He drove his motor home down and spent his time in the mountains of Northern Mexico. He claimed to love the area. In truth he would go down there for a load of cocaine.

Everyone at the border crossing knew he was a cop. He would stop and shoot the breeze with the border guards for a while whenever he went through. No one thought to search his RV. If they had, they would have found several hundred pounds of white death. He got away with his operation for several years. The Department discovered his activity through an informant, and records. If he got caught, he would have some problems, but he would only serve a couple years.

It would cause the DEA, INS, and the Customs service a lot of embarrassment. He had to be stopped, permanently.

I flew under the border radar into Mexico during the dark hours of a heavily overcast sky. By the time the sun came up, we were flying over the cop's campsite. We knew he had just gotten into Mexico and was headed south. The back road he was on didn't have any side roads for nearly fifty miles, so we landed on the road about twenty miles south of his camp.

We got the airplane off the road and into the brush. I left the pilot with the plane and hiked back down the road a good five miles. I was lying on a little knoll, waiting, when the motor home appeared. It was going about forty miles an hour. I gauged the distance and lead switching the rifle to full automatic. When I pulled the trigger three rounds got away before I could react. One slug hit the leading side of the left front tire. Another one hit the hubcap, and the last one hit the back of the tire. I got him with a single shot, when he got out to see what happened to his tire.

Before I got away, a group of six men, riding horses, came out of a dry wash. They stopped at the motor home and, after seeing that the man was dead, began ripping it apart. Two of the men started shooting the dead man and into the vehicle. If he was not already dead, he sure was then. I continued to watch as they took the billfold, watch, and rings. They removed everything they thought they could carry from inside, and set the rest on fire. I knew they had more than likely heard my shots, and would soon be looking for me, so I returned to the airplane quickly. We got out of there before the bandits caught up with us.

The ruins, and body, were not discovered for over a week. When the news got to the papers in the

Northwest, the man had been killed by bandits. The perpetrators were never found.

Our investigation showed that his widow and children never knew of his sideline. They were greatly surprised, and puzzled, at the size of his estate. After taxes, they enjoyed a much better life style than when the Police Captain was living.

When I got back to school, several students asked me how the Fellowship Meeting went. I said "fine" and didn't comment any further. I had not made close friends with the other students. I was either working, or in class, most of the time. No one pressed me for details. The one person who should have been truly interested, the witch, acted as though it was a nuisance to have me back.

I never got another call for my services, until the day I was to graduate. The witch didn't attend the ceremony. She had to "work". Jim wanted to know if I planned to transfer my credits to the college in California. I knew his interest was more than friendship, or curiosity. I told him that I was offered a job as Assistant Pastor of a church in the Bay Area. If he needed me in California, I could accept the position. He concluded our conversation by asking me to meet him at a hotel on Nob Hill, in San Francisco, on a certain date.

In order to get my degree from the college in California, I had to be enrolled as a student. I signed up for two courses. I attended classes for two weeks before challenging both subjects. By "challenging", all I needed was to pass a test on each course. In another week I was awarded an accredited degree.

My previous concerns with my name were taken care of by someone. It seems that when the transcripts for my previous education arrived the name was changed. I got the degree, but under the wrong name.

14.

I was informed that my country needed me for an extended period of time. I was to end my "new life" and resume being myself. Two days later I put into action my own death.

My "wife" had to work late again. She had to "work late" a lot. It started right after she found out that her new boss was divorced. The boys were at a sitter's house, because I informed her that I had an important meeting, and some business to attend. About ten o'clock that night I drove down the coast. There was a spot along the beach that was popular with kids.

When I arrived only one car was parked about a hundred yards from where I was, just away from the water. I could see the young couple watching me through the rain and darkness. I parked my old jalopy and wiped down the steering wheel, rear view mirror and the dash. I then jumped out and ran around to the passenger side. I opened that door and stood behind it while empting all of my pockets. I left everything except my money on the hood of the car. The couple drove away like the cops were after them.

Alone now, I ran up the beach with water washing over my tracks. At a rocky place, I cut away from the water and entered the woods. From there, all I had to do was not being seen until I reached a pre-set rendezvous with Jim two miles up the coast.

It was nearly an hour later that we drove past the spot where I "committed myself to the deep". By that time I had changed clothes. The old ones were in a sack in the trunk of the car, to be disposed of many miles from there. The teen's car was there, along with a police car. We watched, with other curious people as the officer followed the tracks down to the water.

One of the people watching was listening on a scanner when the policeman called in his report. "Some guy just killed himself," the man said.

In the three or so years I lived with the witch we had never had sex and I only kissed her on very rare occasions. I was very sorry for the boys and was sad to leave them. They deserved better than her.

I found out several days later that my death was listed as a homicide. It seems the kids had sworn there were two people in the car and they saw one man dragging the other out of the passenger side. Eyewitnesses are strange. Their testimony was reinforced by the lack of fingerprints on the steering wheel and dash.

15.

By the next night I was in a secret training facility, in the Rocky Mountains. For the next two months I participated in a concentrated school. We had seven students whose profile said they could be of use. We washed out two of them on the second day. Four graduated and were sent out. The last one was a special student.

I had not realized, until this school, that most of my shots had been at very long range. The long-range headshot just behind the ear, with a very small caliber bullet, had become a trademark. The most dangerous thing an assassin could do is to establish a trademark. The shots I had made were in diverse parts of the world, and had not been overly frequent. So far as I knew, no one had made the connection, but I vowed to change that image.

The young man was a good student. We practiced with the rifle that he would be using, twelve hours a day. The weapon was a larger caliber than I was used to using. It carried a 30 caliber cartridge, with a lot of powder. It kicked like a mule, in spite of special recoil devices. It used a very high-powered scope that could pinpoint a target, with a red dot. It adjusted automatically for distance, elevation and windage. It had a couple other features that made it special. We called it the "gismo". I could hit a target, the size of a quarter, at a distance of over two miles. "Gismo" was a special weapon, built for a very special purpose, one job.

After target practice was over, I lectured, and counseled, another three, to five, hours. After another week, I felt he was ready. I called Jim, to tell him that I thought the "kid" could make the shot. I was twenty-three, and calling a man not two, or three, years younger a "kid". I was instructed to keep at it for two more days. That was when his briefing would take place. Both the "kid", and I, would learn why we had been working so diligently.

The briefing was anything but brief. First, we were informed about the target's relationship to organized crime, two murders, and numerous other actions. He had political power, money, and connections to powerful people both in the United States and other countries that kept him from the punishment he deserved. The target had gotten into a position that would enable him to do great harm to the nation, and even the world.

We were told that the opportunity would present itself in ten days. It was then that he told us the identity of the target. I could not believe what I heard. The kid's mouth opened and closed several times. He grew pale and his shoulders dropped as though he was, suddenly, very old and very tired. His target suddenly had a name and identity. He was a charismatic religious and political leader. His country did not have an extradition treaty with the U.S. Law enforcement wanted him for two murders and had solid proof they could do nothing about. There was an extended silence, lasting nearly five minutes. Each of us busy with our own thoughts.

I had "popped a cap" on some pretty important targets. There were leaders of crime, heads of small countries, and others, but this target made the others

184

seem as though they were only paper targets. This one was well known and therefore the best protected. I was sure this was a suicide mission. No one could get away from this one, no matter how good he was. Yet get away was exactly what had to be done. If it was known that an American government agency had done the job all hell would break loose.

The next day, during rifle practice, the kid began to miss. Even a poor shot could hit a quarter at the distance we were using. Our range was nearly two miles. He hit the target perfectly every time, before. Now he missed every time. At the time I called him ready he had had over a hundred perfect tries. He was no longer shooting a piece of paper. He was shooting a person. He was pulling his shots. He missed by two to three inches. That night he rested his chin on the muzzle of the rifle and pulled the trigger.

Not ten minutes after the kid put an end to his own life, I learned that the shot was postponed. The resources of the Department were almost universal. They had discovered that there was another person planning to shoot our target. This individual had come under the eye of various branches of the government, and thus the Department. He was a psychopath with a problem. When he purchased a rifle they knew he had something planned. Fortunately, it was the same caliber as "gismo".

All that remained was to discover his plan and direct him, without him knowing he was being used. He had the ambition, means, and motivation. There was only one problem. He couldn't shoot worth a damn.

The day came. A large number of police and other security personnel as well as a number of dignitaries, some from the United States government, were escorting the target.

The "nut case" started shooting from the second story of a building that bordered the route of the motorcade. For some "unknown" reason the building had not been cleared by security before the motorcade arrived.

The only two men who could handle the job were nearly two miles away. One watched the "Nut" while the other handled the "gismo". When the shooting started, one bullet was fired from the "gismo". It found its mark. The nut got the credit - or the blame. He died before he could be charged and so there was not much of an investigation. It was obvious who was doing the shooting. The sniper had used the windowsill to rest his rifle and the barrel stuck out of the window a good foot. After he shot, he stood there looking, with the rifle in his hand to see if he had been successful. Everyone on the street could clearly see him. The police shot him at the scene. Case closed.

After firing just that one round, the two men disassembled "gismo" and hid the parts down vent pipes, air supply ducts etc. They walked out of the building dressed as construction workers discussing the impending demolition of the building. "Gismo" no longer existed.

16.

I went back to civilian life and started another job. I got recalled and did my job. I went back to civilian life. I got recalled. This happened over and over. In total I was "recalled" 19 times by the time I got that call while I lived in Seattle up on Queen Anne Hill. Arrangements were made. I was on a "sales trip" as far as anyone knew.

Back when I eliminated the two gangsters, from the top of a hill, I started a war that lasted two and a half years. Eventually, one man became the leader of both groups. That leader also became the Dictator of his country. The major exports of that South American country were cocaine and marijuana, and most of them went to the United States. The CIA had tried to get a revolution going, but this individual was too strong. The "War on Drugs" program had been useless, and helpless.

The CIA and DEA "blew it", but they had given the Department some valuable information. When their intelligence was compared to that of other sources, it was determined that the Dictator was not, actually, in charge. The one behind the scenes was the person who was the real power. Six months of hard work went into the project before it was decided that the "office" should be advised.

One of the villas I had seen through my scope was now occupied by my target. A satellite photograph showed that the hill had changed considerably. There were gun emplacements, bunkers, and a large number of men occupying that hill. In addition, an electric fence surrounded the villa, with surveillance cameras, walking patrols inside and out, and guard towers. Since the target seldom left the villa, I would have to go to him.

The most heavily guarded section of the fence was only four hundred yards from the house. I wanted a closer look, so we enlarged that portion of the photograph. There was plenty of undergrowth to provide cover, but I could plainly see three patrols, of four men each, outside of the fence. That area seemed to be out.

Another possibility was where the fence crossed a stream, but there was a permanent guard post at that location. The front gate looked like the entrance to the Gold Room at Fort Knox. The more I studied the situation, the more impossible it looked and the more intrigued I was with the mission. I needed to prove to myself that I deserved my reputation.

I was receiving as many as six pictures a day. Nothing changed, until the first day of the month. On that day a large number of peasants gathered at the main gate. One photograph showed my target and the Dictator handing out money to those people. The Department's files confirmed that this was a monthly occurrence. It was payday. In fact, CIA operatives had tried to get the revolution going by having dissidents start a riot, and shoot the Dictator, on the first of a month. No one had the nerve to take the first shot so the operation failed.

As in all Dictatorships the few have all the wealth, while the many suffer poverty. This creates a very unhappy populace. In this instance they were still too afraid to do something about the situation.

The CIA even had the new "President" for the country picked. He promised to eliminate the drug trade, in exchange for foreign aid to get the country's legitimate businesses going and start schools. The Department got the CIA to have as many revolutionaries as they could muster there at the first of the next month. They were told that their revolution would be successfully started.

Four days before the first of the month I was flown into the country the same way as the previous time. This time I took a different route with the motor scooter. It took two nights, sleeping days, to get to my destination. I arrived after midnight, having walked the last three miles. The first thing I did was to hide from a patrol. If they had not been talking about something I would have walked right into them. I was far enough away, when I heard them, to slip into the brush.

I silently worked my way up to a position where I could judge the distance to the platform the "Big Wheels" used when they paid their people. From there I retreated to a tall tree. It was only a little over two hundred yards from the platform. I found that it had a lot of leaves and branches to hide me, when I climbed high enough.

I stashed some of my gear under a bush and sprinkled leaves over the pack. I took one radio-controlled tape player and started to my right. I had walked about three steps when I caught a movement out of the corner of my eye. I dropped to the ground and quietly worked my way to concealment. Listening closely, I heard steps, both to my right and to my left. The footsteps to my right were quieter and now and then I heard a branch move. I looked. It was a deer. To my left I heard some whispered words, then someone approaching.

I didn't understand the language but I was sure someone had said "what's that". Another replied, "go check it out", or "go see". The man nearly stepped on my hand. I had to close my fist to prevent him from crushing my fingers. I was sure I was caught when the deer became frightened and bounded off. The guard turned around while he stood within arm's reach of me and said something. I thought it was, "It's only a deer".

Another voice, to my left, laughed and said something. I waited until I couldn't hear the patrol's footsteps before I moved again. I crawled nearly a hundred yards before I placed the tape player under some bushes, and covered it with leaves. Covering my trail, and crawling that distance, while being quiet and alert took nearly two hours. Once away from the tape player I took the risk of moving on my feet. I slipped from one cover to another.

When I got back to my tree, I picked up the other tape player and started in the opposite direction to place the other one. This one was easier to place, but on the way back I met either another patrol or the same one. Three men were sitting on a log smoking cigarettes and talking. I walked past, not ten feet behind them. Placing that second unit only took an hour.

By dawn I was up the tree, with the rest of my gear. People started arriving at the crack of dawn. From my information, I knew the money would not be passed out until nearly noon. I assembled my rifle. It was the same one I had used on the previous mission. I had to climb a little further before I could get a clear view of the platform. Once I was prepared, I made myself as comfortable as possible and waited. The crowd woke me from a light sleep.

I could see the Dictator and my target coming toward their platform. There were three high-ranking military officer with them and about fifty troops. A table was set up and stacks of money were placed on it. There was a slight breeze, so rocks were placed on the stacks, to keep the money from being blown away. The Dictator started the program off by making a speech.

He had talked about fifteen minutes when I noticed that the crowd was starting to get "ancy". There was a shuffling of feet and murmuring. All of the workers had assembled close to the gate so I was behind them by quite a distance. It was my turn to "entertain" the workers. The silencer would help keep my location secret and the lack of sound would confuse everyone.

The first round took my target just above the left ear. He didn't even fall. He just slumped down in his chair as though he had fallen asleep. Everyone on the platform stood there as though frozen in place. The Dictator had quit talking, but his mouth was still moving. My next bullet hit him in the forehead, an inch above where his eyebrows met. He went over backward. Just then I hit the switch on my little transmitter. There was shouting from two sides. I don't know the words, but I know about what was being said. "Hurray for the Revolution . . . Kill the Dictators . . . Kill them all . . . Etc." I shot one of the generals before he got off the stage. He fell and knocked over the table. The wind caught the money and started blowing it all over the place. The remaining two officers started shouting orders. Both of them had to die before the crowd started to act. It was a short battle, but a bloody one. All of the soldiers, and guards, were killed, and a great number of the peasants. I sat in my tree and watched the scene below me. It was the safest place to hide, yet bullets hit the branches around me, several times.

There was a second man on my "hit list" that day. It was the CIA's new "President". The Department had information on him that went back several years. He was a Cuban Marxist, trained in Russia. I spotted him near the end of the battle. I had not seen him earlier. I figured that he "arrived late". He was shouting and acting like a leader. He even wore a uniform, complete with medals. The CIA would think it was too bad their man got killed in the first battle. I didn't know, or care, who would wind up taking over the country. Whoever it was would not be any worse that his predecessor, or the CIA's pick.

The gun emplacements, up on the hill, started booming away when the villa was set on fire, but they soon fell silent. I assumed that the revolutionaries had reached the ridge. When it became dark the people dispersed. I got down from my tree and started back toward my motor scooter.

It was not easy getting the kinks out of my body. After sitting on a tree limb for so long I was pretty sore. Better than being dead, but I felt like my legs would fall off. I quit limping after the first mile. As I walked along I could see the glow of fires and hear the sounds of battle. The revolution had spread. My fears that my transportation may have been discovered were unfounded. By dawn I was far away.

I stopped for the day in a grove of trees, near a stream. The brush was so thick that I had a difficult time entering it. There was no way to completely hide my trail into that patch. About three in the afternoon I heard someone talking excitedly. When I peeked through the bushes, I saw a young soldier pointing at my trail and talking to at least one other man. On an order, he started toward me.

The soft puff of my rifle sounded, to me, like a cannon, but evidently no one else heard it. When he fell, I heard at least two other voices. At first they laughed, and said something, as though they thought he had stumbled. When he didn't get up they started into the brush, to see what was wrong. They found out. I heard at least one other person run away, in fright. I decided it was time to get out of there.

Although I was on nothing more than a path through the woods, I still had to drop six more soldiers, and one revolutionary, before I got to the landing field. It was early in the evening when I arrived at the field so I hid in the brush and waited for my ride out of there.

I watched three Army patrols cross the field, all going the same direction. Behind the last patrol, about fifteen revolutionaries trailed them. Later, I heard gunfire and then, an hour later, I saw the fifteen men return, laden with the arms and ammunition of the soldiers.

Just at dusk my light aircraft came to pick me up. I started riding the scooter toward the plane before it landed. Revolutionaries began to chase me, shooting. I waived the plane away and committed myself to my fate. He didn't pull up. He landed the craft. The airplane was still moving when I threw the rifle and my backpack into the machine and jumped on. The scooter was still moving when I left it. It became our contribution to the war effort. I don't know who won that war, but I do know that the drug supply from that country dried up, for over a year.

That pilot saved my life. His orders were to leave me there, if there was trouble. He didn't do it. I did not even know his name. He had flown me on the previous mission into that area, and on other occasions, but we never exchanged more than ten words.

When we landed I counted at least 30 bullet holes in his light aircraft. We had been pure luck none of them hit anything vital on us or on the plane.

I met him again several years later, he was dying of emphysema. We became good friends, but we never mentioned our previous experiences. We both knew why we were friends. A year after his funeral I told his wife part of the reason. She said she had suspected something like that. Her husband had taken off, on mysterious missions, many times. She was certain he worked for the government, in some capacity, but he would never confide in her.

I got the target that could not be reached, but it was not that difficult. I had imagined that it would be very complicated. I still did not think I deserved the reputation Jim insisted on giving me.

I have to admit I was not all that bad either. In 34 different missions I got my target 34 times. I was a soldier doing his job and nothing more. It was no different than a soldier in combat. I was one among hundreds of thousands that served his or her country. There was nothing special about me at all.

To this day when I hear the Star Spangled Banner or the Pledge of Allegiance I swell up with pride and many times a tear can be seen in my eye.

17.

Before I went back to Seattle Jim and I had a conversation. I told him I was about to get married and I would have to quit. He told me he had others that could handle the job but he may still have to call on me at some point. He never called on me for nearly ten years and that was a quick local job. I was able to disguise my absence from home under the cover of a union safety meeting. I was the Safety Officer for my local union.

My wife and I were separated when Jim "recalled" me to go to Portland. I drove down and spent a day and a night taking care of a little problem for him. That was one of the Arian Nation people that died without a lot of publicity after being fouled up by federal agencies. It got no publicity to speak of at all.

I never got recalled again until after I married again and moved to Texas. It was just after the first Gulf War started. My wife got a strange call and told me about it. I called and told Jim I could no longer handle what he wanted but I could instruct his shooter. I never had to leave my job but a couple of days and had the cooperation of my boss. We met at a ranch some ten or so miles from my home and I told their man what to do. A drug dealer in South America was killed "by rivals" a couple of days later and a plot to send narcotics to our troops over in the Middle East was stopped. I made Lt. Colonel for my participation. I was told at the time that when I retired I would be able to retire at my military rank with military retirement. I was to receive one year's credit for each time I was recalled plus my service time. That would have given me 26 years. I trusted that it would happen. I was wrong.

When I was recalled for the final time my wife had died and my son was out of college. I had been judged by the Social Security Administration as disabled and not able to work because of several ailments. I got recalled and sent to a base in Kansas for indoctrination and orientation. This was a legitimate recall.

The first day I got my orders. I was now a full Colonel. I saw my service record for the first time. I had a whole bunch of medals I didn't know about. I noticed that I was still in MI and was an auditor, according to the record.

Jim was there and we went out to celebrate. By then he was a Lieutenant General and had already put in his papers to retire. There was a Lieutenant Colonel, who would be my second in command, with us. A Captain and a First Lieutenant who would also be in the unit were there as well. We all got to feeling pretty good that night.

We got to discussing, or rather cussing, our current Commander In Chief. I may have said something about putting an extra hole in his head, or something of that nature. They all drank to the idea. I did say I would never do it unless ordered to do so.

I had been given a training command. We would train a unit of some two hundred and fifty career enlisted men in covert operations. Not the gung-ho, kick-ass tough type like the Special Service or Rangers. These men would operate under the radar with skill and cunning without making any waves. Every one of the men would have an IQ of 125 or higher.

On the second day I was starting to acquire my uniforms and other gear. I was told they didn't have my size in stock and to come back in a couple of days.

On the morning of the third day I was sent for a physical. I was sitting on the side of an exam table when the young doctor, a Captain, who had given me my physical, came in and told me. "Sir, put you clothes on a go home. We can't use you."

I was hoping I would pass that physical in spite of having a bad heart, three hernias, emphysema and a nervous condition that makes me shake a little. After all, my new job didn't require me to do a damn thing but sit behind a desk and give orders. The Army saw it differently.

I went home after helping Jim celebrate his retirement. I was given the task of typing up the lesson plans for the operation. I had them all done and on computer discs. I called to have them picked up and delivered. I was told to destroy the discs. He said some politician had found out about the operation and called it all off. Only one politician could do that.

In just a few days my records were looked over and I was given one year's credit for each year I was recalled instead of each time, as promised. I wound up with far too few years to retire from the military. I never got the chance to argue about that. My service record went back into the highly classified files. Jim tried to get my retirement for me but his efforts hit a stone wall.

Just before he left office our "Esteemed" Commander In Chief eliminated our job in the agency, accidentally or otherwise I don't know. We no longer existed and had never existed. Jim got his retirement because he retired before that man left office.

I got zilch.

AUTHORS NOTE

Is this a true story?

Make up your own mind.

Jim, if he still lives, is in his 90's and is in Idaho somewhere. I am between 69 and 75 and live in Montana. We are the only two living people who know for sure, with the possible exception of a politician.

If the story is true isn't it dangerous to tell it?

Who Cares?

www.ingramcontent.com/pod-product-compliance
Lightning Source LLC
Chambersburg PA
CBHW060935180626
46817CB00004B/1563